An excerpt from The Realm:

The thunder subsided momentarily, and they heard the roar of waterfalls on the cloud-veiled slopes below.

The curious excitement and anticipation that Andrew had been feeling all day reached its zenith on the mountaintop, and he trembled with joy. Sheer elation. Far from being intimidated by the surreal sights and sounds, he wanted nothing more than to run full speed downhill, into the strange, foreign land. Because truth be told, at that moment, it did not feel strange or foreign at all. It felt familiar. Welcoming. As if he'd seen it before. As if it'd been beckoning to him for years. Since earliest childhood.

Andrew turned from the Eden below and looked at his father, who clearly was not having the same kind of experience. The man appeared terrified. Eyes wide. Jaw slack. He whipped around—pivoting 180 degrees in a series of jerking half steps, tossing powder into the air with his snowshoes—and stared in the opposite direction. Andrew did the same. The view this way had not changed.

Wanderings: A Collection of Six Short Stories
by

Kenneth G. Bennett

Wanderings: A Collection of Six Short Stories

Cover Art by *Kristian Norris*

The Wild Rose Press, Inc.
PO Box 708
Adams Basin, NY 14410-0708
Visit us at www.thewildrosepress.com

Publishing History
First Edition, 2022
Trade Paperback ISBN 978-1-5092-4052-4
Digital ISBN 978-1-5092-4053-1

Published in the United States of America

Dedication

For my family

The Guide

Wanderings

The Guide watched the family enter the farmers' market from the west—from Lawrence Street. A man and a woman in their late thirties or early forties and a girl, age six or seven. The family merged with the sauntering Saturday crowd, staying together, pausing at various stalls to admire the goods within—colorful summer produce, fresh-baked breads, flowers, bright and vibrant. They sampled artisan cheeses at one stall— the Guide couldn't see if they purchased anything—and tested the handmade Adirondack chairs in another. The little girl seemed almost to disappear into the chair she tried. Her dad helped her climb back out. They all laughed.

They were taking their time, taking it all in, enjoying the sunny July day. But they were getting closer.

The Guide waited.

To the casual observer, the family looked fine. Healthy. Happy. Complete.

The Guide knew otherwise.

Beneath the veneer, despite their best efforts, the little family bore a wound that would not heal, would never heal—not if they all lived to be one hundred. The parents carried the bulk of the burden, but the little girl felt it, as well. The hurt permeated everything. Colored everything.

They were approaching the Guide's part of the market now—the little girl in the lead, twirling like a ballerina, singing to herself, lost in her own daydream, the parents following, holding hands.

They came on and drew even with the Guide.

The Guide's "stall"—if you could call it that—was by far the simplest in the market, consisting of a folding chair and a section of cedar log placed on end for a table.

The couple noticed it at the same time and paused, ten feet away. The little girl stopped dancing.

The Guide got to his feet. Smiled. The woman smiled back, then read the hand-lettered sign propped on the cedar log: *Explore Olympic National Park with an experienced, licensed guide. Half-day, full-day, and overnight outings. Ask for details.*

"Let me know if I can answer any questions," said the Guide, wondering if they would notice his accent.

"You work for a company?" asked the man.

"For myself," replied the Guide. "I've spent most of my life in the mountains."

The family kept their distance and stared at the sign longer than they needed to, as if trying to discern some deeper meaning in the simple offer.

The Guide waited.

Bluegrass music wafted from a far corner of the market, the sound of a lone fiddle cutting through the hum of the crowd. The woman lifted her eyes from the sign and stared at the Guide. He held her gaze. Thought he saw the briefest flicker of recognition—an instant of knowing—dismissed, discarded, as suddenly as it had flashed to mind.

Just a flicker.

And now the family was moving on, toward the metalworker's stall and booths displaying glasswork, organic-fiber clothing, handmade lotions and soaps.

The Guide watched and noticed that their pace had changed. They were moving more slowly now. Talking. The woman was gesturing. Maybe trying to make a point.

The Guide saw the woman glance back his way.

He waited.

And prayed.

****

"He looks too old," said the man.

"He looks like he could out-hike us," said his wife, laughing.

"We don't need a guide for that trail, Laura."

"Yes. We do. *Especially* for that trail."

****

It took fifteen minutes for the family to return. This time, they emerged from the crowd and walked right up to the Guide.

"I'm Paul Wagner," said the man. "This is my wife, Laura, and this is our daughter, Jenny."

"Graham Evans," said the Guide as he shook their hands. "Nice to meet you folks."

"We don't really need a guide," said Paul.

The Guide nodded respectfully. "I see."

"We live here. We're not tourists. We've hiked all over the Olympics. Day hikes. Long backpacking trips. We know what we're doing."

"I'm sure you do."

Laura said, "But we have a trip in mind for tomorrow, a day hike where we feel like we might really benefit from …," she hesitated. "From having someone with us."

"I see," replied the Guide. "Where are you folks

3

thinking of hiking tomorrow?"

"Marmot Pass," Paul replied. "An easy one. We've done it a bunch of times. In fact…"

"Daddy," Jenny said, "isn't that where Ryan … you know …?"

Laura pulled the little girl to her side and held her close. "Hush," she whispered.

"Our son died on Marmot Pass," Laura told the Guide. Her voice was steady, but her face had gone a little pale. "Five years ago."

"I'm so sorry."

"Maybe you heard the story. It was all over the news for weeks. There was a big search."

"Yes," he said gently. "I do remember that."

"We haven't been back. We haven't been to the mountains at all since then. But we think it's time."

The Guide nodded, his weatherworn face full of compassion. "I think I understand," he said. "And I'd be honored to accompany you—if you like."

"A mountain lion ate Ryan," Jenny said matter-of-factly.

"Sweetie," her mother countered, "we don't know what happened to Ryan." Then, to the Guide, "Our little boy was never found. He wandered away and…"

"Will there be mountain lions when we go?" blurted Jenny, peering up at the Guide, meeting his glacier-blue eyes with an innocence and directness that utterly disarmed him.

The Guide squatted down so that he was eye level with the child. "We'll stay together tomorrow, Jenny," he said. "No animals will bother us. You don't have to worry about that."

****

They talked about gear. Logistics. Cost. And agreed to meet at the trailhead at eight the following morning.

The family said goodbye, and the Guide watched them go.

Tough, resilient, lean and hard as an old alpha wolf, few things perturbed the Guide. Now, though, watching the family melt into the crowd, his hands shook. His heart hammered in his chest.

****

They met the next morning at the agreed-upon place—the Big Quilcene River trailhead at the end of US Forest Service Road 2750. The Guide was standing under an old-growth Douglas fir tree near the self-service kiosk when they arrived—weathered pack on his back, stout walking stick in his right hand.

"Looks like John Muir is ready to go," said Paul as he parked the car.

Laura laughed. "Paul …"

"Who's John Muir?" Jenny asked from the back seat. "I thought his name was Graham."

"It is, sweetie," said her mother. "Daddy's being silly. John Muir was a famous naturalist."

"What's a naturalist?"

"Someone who knows a lot about nature. Animals, plants, insects."

"Oh."

"'Natural' is a good word for him." Paul peered through the windshield. "His gear looks homemade."

It did. The Guide's pack, walking stick, even his boots—all looked as patinaed as their owner. Original. Handcrafted.

"A little eccentric," said Laura. "But I like him. He

5

reminds me of someone I knew a long time ago."

"Who?" asked Paul.

Laura shook her head. Laughed. "I can't remember. It's driving me crazy."

****

Paul filled out a hiking permit and marked the group's destination as Marmot Pass—five point three miles in.

Laura stood alongside her husband, scanning the maps and official notices tacked to the kiosk. Warnings to treat all drinking water, camp in designated areas only, keep food in bear-proof containers, and the like. She said quietly, "Ryan helped me fill out the permit that day. He was standing right here next to me. Just like we're standing now."

Paul stopped writing and set down the pen. Looked at her. Took her hands gently in his. "You okay with this? We don't have to do this hike."

"I'm fine," she replied. "And we *need* to do this hike."

****

Car locked, packs loaded and ready, they turned their backs to civilization and plunged into the primeval forest. There was no one else around. The trail—broad and well maintained—climbed gradually but steadily from the start.

The gloom of the cathedral grove deepened, and they traveled in silence, adjusting to the trail, to their packs, to each other, falling into a rhythm—the Big Quilcene River rolling and rumbling like drums in the distance.

They walked past hulking hemlocks, colossal firs, cedars hundreds of years old and hundreds of feet tall.

Over brawling streams and around house-size boulders clothed in moss.

"The glaciers left these here," the Guide told Jenny as they approached one of the massive boulders, "thousands of years ago."

Jenny stopped—they all stopped—and studied the huge stone. Water dripped from the moss, and the rock beneath glistened in the muted light.

"Ryan loved climbing on these," Paul murmured, running his hand over the stone. Feeling the moss. "Took forever to hike anywhere with that boy."

Laura laughed. "It sure did—but that was part of the fun."

****

They saw no one and encountered no wildlife, save for birds flitting through the shadows—wrens and jays, warblers and woodpeckers.

The miles passed.

At 4,000 feet, the forest gave way to avalanche chutes and vast scree slopes fanning down from Buckhorn and Iron Mountains. They stopped next to a stream to rest and eat a snack.

"Maybe Ryan's still here," said Jenny, eyeing a stand of stunted trees on the opposite slope. She was sitting on the ground, shoes off, one foot splashing in the stream—eating gummy bears, one bear at a time. "He could be. Since they never found him."

The adults exchanged glances.

The Guide said, "Do you remember your brother, Jenny?"

She shook her head. "Sort of. Not really. I was still a baby. I wish I did."

****

They hiked on, winding their way uphill, Jenny and Paul in front, the Guide and Laura a couple of minutes behind.

"We brought a tent for the kids to nap in," Laura told the Guide after a long silence. "It was just a day hike, but it was late October, so we had warm clothes and the backpacking stove—for soup and hot chocolate. Ryan was six, Jenny, eighteen months—Paul carried her pretty much the whole way. She liked riding on his back. Ryan did, too, when he was that age."

They crossed another stream and entered Camp Mystery. It was deserted. No people. No tents—unusual for July.

"I remember it was chilly when we got here," Laura continued. "But exhilarating—like fall can be. You know?" She stopped walking and regarded the Guide with a sad, slightly self-conscious smile. "Do you mind if I talk? It feels good to talk about this stuff—especially here."

"I don't mind at all," he replied gently. "I'd like to hear the story."

Laura said, "The searchers used Camp Mystery as a staging area. Some came in by helicopter and landed on the ridge. Others hiked up the trail. There must have been fifteen tents here. More near the pass."

****

The trail zigzagged higher, around vast outcroppings of basalt, and they left Camp Mystery far below. Laura talked. She told the Guide about the search-and-rescue teams, the tracking dogs, the friends, relatives, and volunteers who trekked in to help.

Now the land opened around them, the last stands of trees giving way to broad meadows iridescent with flowers.

The Big Quilcene valley lay spread out below—Puget Sound in the distance, and beyond the sound, Glacier Peak. The Cascades. It was a stunningly clear day—to the east.

To the west, where Paul and Jenny had just reached the grassy saddle of Marmot Pass, the sky was dark and full of fat, gray clouds.

****

Laura and the Guide stopped at a junction a short distance below the pass, where a side trail led due north to a flat, grassy bench tucked into the side of the ridge. The bench was dominated by an enormous boulder, broken into two jagged halves.

The boulder lay there. Dramatic. Raw. A bit of detritus left thousands of years earlier by retreating ice. The rock had undoubtedly weathered over the centuries, yet it looked somehow new. Alive. As if it had just that morning been born, then blasted in half by some stupendous bolt of lightning. Or smashed by a giant's sledgehammer.

Laura eyed the stone uneasily. "Ryan spotted that when we were hiking in five years ago," she said. "He wanted to explore, but I wouldn't let him. Paul and I just wanted to get to the pass and eat lunch. We were tired and worried about running out of daylight. October, you know? When we realized Ryan was missing, that's the first place we looked. I ran straight here."

She stared at the granite behemoth, remembering. "There was just a trace of snow on the ground. A light dusting on the grass. I thought I saw footprints—just the faintest little impressions around the rock, leading into that fissure between the two pieces. But I was wrong—he wasn't there. I called and called and looked all around. So did everyone else."

****

All four hikers reconvened on Marmot Pass, opening packs and adding layers of clothing against the steady, chill wind. Massive clouds obscured Mount Fricaba and Mount Deception to the west and were closing fast on the Needles, engulfing the jagged peaks with silent, flowing tentacles of fog. The entire length of the Upper Dungeness valley lay in shadow.

Paul laughed. "Gotta love the weather in the Olympics. The forecast called for sun. Just sun."

"We should eat lunch," said Laura, "before it rains. Or maybe it'll all clear off here in a little bit. Either way, I'm hungry."

"Me, too," said Jenny. "I'm starving. There are more gummy bears, right?"

Paul smiled and mussed his daughter's hair. "There *might* be more gummy bears—if you eat a good lunch."

****

They found a shallow, grassy bowl somewhat sheltered from the wind a few hundred yards above the pass, with views all around. They sat on the ground, talking softly, watching the sky morph and rearrange itself, like a sky in a time-lapse film. Great billowing clouds tumbled into the Dungeness Valley, getting closer. The breeze picked up.

Peering over the edge, Laura spotted Boulder Shelter on the Upper Dungeness Trail, a thousand feet below the ridge. She watched as the shelter vanished under the eclipse-like shadow of the advancing storm.

"Not very summery," she said. "No wonder there

are no other people."

She regarded her companions and smiled. Raised her voice over the wind. "It's all good, though. Even if it rains, I'm glad we're here. Glad we did this. And Graham—I'm happy you're with us."

"Me, too," he replied, eyes riveted on the wild sky.

Laura said, "I was telling Paul, I feel like I know you—like we've met before."

The Guide said nothing for several seconds. The wind howled around them.

"We *have* met before," he said.

They looked at him curiously. "When?" asked Paul, a bite of sandwich in his mouth.

The Guide stood and walked to the lip of the shallow bowl. There was a faint amethyst tint to the clouds now, and it looked like the midday sun would soon be obscured.

"The trail we just hiked," said the Guide, "I first took it sixty-one years ago—with my family."

"That's amazing," said Paul. "How many times have you done it since then?"

"Once. Three weeks ago. When I hiked back out."

Paul raised an eyebrow. "Hiked back out?"

"I came here sixty-one years ago," said the Guide, facing them, "and sat on this ridge with my mother and father and sister. And then I went down the hill—just for a minute—and I couldn't get back. Couldn't find them again. I tried and tried, but there was no way. Not until three weeks ago, when it opened back up."

The Guide studied the tumultuous sky once more, concern in his eyes. "Things are changing again. Sooner than I'd hoped. I don't have much time."

Paul set his sandwich back in its Tupperware

container. Tapped his wife with his foot.

"You feeling okay, Graham?" Paul asked.

The Guide made no reply.

Paul said, "You're saying you've been in the mountains for sixty-one years?"

"Yes. And no. Here, but not exactly here."

The Guide's eyes flicked between the sky and the fractured boulder on the ridge's lower flank.

Laura said, "You mentioned we'd met before. When?"

The Guide knelt and regarded her for a long moment. "In your dream, most recently. When you dreamed about the farmers' market. I held your hand and asked you to come to Port Townsend."

Laura's entire body twitched, as if she'd touched a live wire. Her eyes went wide. "*Ryan* held my hand," she said.

"Yes."

"How did you …? I'd forgotten that dream until this second."

Jenny twisted closer to her father in the grass. "I'm scared, Daddy."

Paul stared at his wife and the Guide. "What's he talking about? What's going on?"

The Guide ignored him. Kept his eyes on Laura. "You told me when we were walking up here that you brought a tent for the kids—the day Ryan went missing."

She nodded.

"It was a Mountain Hardwear tent," he said. "Big thing. Kind of a burnt-orange color but fading."

"I didn't tell you that."

The Guide glanced at Paul. "You said it was fading

because of the UV light. You were talking about getting a new one. I didn't know what 'UV light' meant, but you explained it to me."

Paul gaped.

"The zippers would always stick," said the Guide. "I remember that. And the big gear pocket in the back was torn. From when you left your Swiss Army knife open accidentally."

Paul Wagner was getting to his feet now, scattering the remains of his sandwich, face flushed and angry. "What is this? How do you know this stuff? Do you know something about Ryan? Did you *do* something to Ryan?"

The Guide remained kneeling in front of Laura and shut his eyes. "You unrolled a sleeping bag for us to lie on, inside the tent. And that blanket Grandma Ellen made. The one with the ducks. It was cozy. You gave me a book and told me to read to Jenny. A book about penguins …"

"Puffins," Laura whispered.

"Puffins," he repeated. "That's right. *There once was a puffin … just the shape of a muffin.*" The Guide opened his eyes and looked at Laura. "I'm sorry I left the tent. I had to pee. You guys were making hot chocolate or something. Looking at the mountains. At the snow. You didn't see me. I saw the split-open rock down the hill and decided to go look at it. Just for a minute. I was planning to come right back."

The Guide heard a click and felt cold metal pressing against the side of his head.

"What did you do to my son?" Paul screamed, voice blending with the shriek of the wind.

"Paul," Laura cried. "No! Put down the gun."

The Guide got slowly to his feet, hands out, in a gesture of peace. Surrender. He faced Paul.

"I thought," said the Guide, "when I got back that you would be dead. Or very old. So much time has passed. But then I discovered it isn't the same here. Time isn't the same. It's only been five years."

Paul shrieked, "What did you do to my son?"

"I have a family of my own," said the Guide. "A wife. Three children. Seven grandchildren."

"And you are never going to see any of them again unless you tell me who the hell you really are."

Laura was at her husband's side now. "Paul, put the gun away."

The Guide moved his right hand to his left forearm, slowly, and began rolling up his sleeve. "The Gordons still have those dogs?"

There was an ugly white scar on his left bicep. A distinctive crescent shape, just above the elbow. Laura and Paul stared at the scar. The gun shook in Paul's hand.

The Guide looked at Laura. "You cried more than I did, I think. You thought I'd lose my arm, remember? But it wasn't that bad. Nineteen stitches. No nerve damage like you feared. Dr. Frankland did a good job."

"Who are you?" Paul asked again, lowering the gun, his voice a weak whisper now.

The Guide faced his mother and father. Laura was sobbing, her entire body shaking. Paul's face was as pale as a ghost's.

"Look at me," said the Guide. "See me. You know who I am."

****

The family stood together in front of the broken

stone, the wind blowing steadily, the clouds the color of bruised skin. Rain was falling, but shafts of sunlight pierced the thick canopy, bathing patches of the ridge in a shimmering, holy aura.

"The boulder exists in two places," said the Guide. "This world and the world I grew up in. It's split in half on that side, too." He looked at his family. "I came back to the rock every year. Camped nearby. Walked the cut, hoping the way might open again, as it did all those years ago. But it never did. Not until three weeks ago."

Laura took his hand. "When you went through, the first time—you were so little." Tears welled in her eyes.

The Guide nodded. "Yes. But people found me. Kind people. Good people. They took me in, explained what had happened. They're a bit more open to this kind of … magic? Phenomenon? Whatever you want to call it. On that side. A family let me stay with them. Gave me a new name. I found my place. Grew up, healthy and strong." He looked at them. "But I never forgot my real family."

"Is it just like here?" asked Paul. "Where you grew up?"

The Guide shook his head. "It's quieter. Fewer machines. Less technology. Not as many people. It's more peaceful. Not to say there aren't disagreements. Wars, even. But less than here."

He faced the stone. The light was changing again. A shaft of sunlight was drifting toward the boulder, like a spotlight searching for a runaway. The Guide took a step into the cut. "There isn't much time."

Jenny took the Guide's hand. "Can we come with you?" she asked. "I want to see it."

He knelt so that he was eye level with the child and

spoke gently. "I believe you could. But you would not be able to return home." He glanced at Paul and Laura. "At least not in a predictable fashion. The door might open again. But it might not. It might never open again."

"We'd be trapped over there," said Paul.

The Guide nodded. "You could build a new life. I would help you. Others would help. You would make friends. But you would be turning your back on everything here. Walking away from all that you have and all that you know."

The Guide started toward the cut. He glanced back, smiling, rain falling around him, sunlight hitting the raindrops—making them glint and glitter like diamonds. "Goodbye."

Another three steps and he began to fade.

The family gasped. They could see *through* him now, see the stone on the other side of his body. And then he was gone, like a wisp of smoke.

Laura looked at Paul and Jenny, and understanding passed between them. Holding hands, they began to walk.

The Knocking Box

Wanderings

The conference room was clean, quiet, air-conditioned. One of many such rooms inside the big modern office building. A visitor arriving via the warmly decorated lobby would never suspect that the kill floor lay just a few feet away. Down a corridor. Behind a soundproof wall. No off-putting odors or troubling sounds penetrated the conference room. No blood sullied the carpet.

The room was generic corporate America. Whiteboards on the walls. Twenty or so chairs around a massive oak table. Pitchers of water on a little cart.

Only five chairs were in use. The two consultants—Brian Wiggs and Shelly Johnson—sat on one side of the table. Senior Vice President of Production Irvin Bosch and two subordinates—Phil McKenna and Otis Underwood—sat on the other.

Wiggs gestured to the monitor on the wall. "Our agenda for today," he said. He was only two slides into his PowerPoint, and already Bosch was fiddling with his phone.

Bosch looked up from his device. Squinted at the PowerPoint. Frowned. "What's this? I thought you were showing us plans. Revisions for the kill floor."

"We're working on the plans and will present those next month," said Wiggs. "Per the schedule. We're here today because we stumbled onto something during our research phase—something we thought you should know about."

Bosch grunted and resumed checking his phone. "Make it quick. I've got a lot on my plate."

Wiggs offered a small, tight smile. "You bet. Thanks for the heads-up." He flipped to the next slide, a schematic showing the holding pens, the crowd pen, and the entrance to the serpentine. "As you'll recall, we set up scanners throughout this section as part of our fact-finding to help us gather some baseline metrics and better understand what's happening to the animals."

Bosch laughed. "'Better understand what's happening to the animals'? We *know* what's happening to the animals. They're being turned into hamburger." McKenna and Underwood chortled along with their boss.

Johnson said, "Yes. But something on the line isn't working, right? That's why you called us. Because of the recent … issues?"

Bosch's expression hardened as Wiggs scrolled through press accounts of escapes from the slaughterhouse—cows going berserk and breaking out of the line, fleeing into nearby fields and farms and attracting the attention of area residents.

One escaped cow had managed to elude plant officials and police for days and was only recaptured with the help of thermal imaging equipment deployed from a helicopter. Much to Bosch's and the other executives' chagrin, the capture was witnessed by townspeople—including children—and the cow, dubbed "Bebe Jean" by a reporter, had become an instant celebrity. The mayor gave Bebe Jean the key to the city. Someone opened a Twitter account, and the cow gained 60,000 followers overnight. The townspeople held a fundraiser to buy Bebe Jean from

Happy Valley and spare her life, and money poured in from around the country—more than enough to save the cow and send her to an animal sanctuary in Madison, Wisconsin.

The Bebe Jean incident had been an embarrassment for the company and a giant headache for Bosch. "What's going on in production?" Bosch's superiors wanted to know. "How is it that we managed to slaughter 2,000 cows a day for twenty years without incident, and now, suddenly we're encountering problems?" Bosch got the message, loud and clear. Management wanted the problems fixed. *Yesterday.* Wanted order restored to the line. And they were holding him accountable.

Wiggs flipped to a wide shot of the kill floor. "We wanted to see what's happening with the animals' emotions as they move along the line. Where does the anxiety begin? Outside, when they're coming off the trucks? In the holding pens? The crowd pen? The serpentine?"

Johnson continued. "We set up scanners along the entire route to monitor blood pressure, adrenal activity, brainwave patterns."

"Brainwave patterns?" Bosch shook his head. "I'm paying for fucking bovine MRIs now?"

Wiggs ignored the remark. "As we've discussed, our contention is that if we can accurately plot the emotions of the animals, we may be able to effectively modify the journey through the kill floor."

"You mentioned you stumbled onto something," said Underwood. "What?"

Wiggs flipped to a bar graph, and Johnson narrated. "We installed the scanners three months ago, and, as you can see, anxiety levels have increased system-wide throughout that time period. Broader fear in the herd beginning earlier in the process. A marked rise in mean blood pressure coupled with an increase in cortisol production and intensified beta wave activity among virtually all of the animals."

"But here's the issue," said Wiggs. "The thing we didn't anticipate. The increased anxiety isn't just among the animals."

Bosch raised an eyebrow. "Say what?"

"The scanners are set wide," explained Johnson, "to capture as many animals as possible. We didn't intend for the instruments to measure neural activity among your workers, but that data *was* captured."

Bosch stared at the consultants. "The workers," he said flatly. "You're doing brain scans on our workers?"

"The scans aren't harmful," replied Wiggs. "And, as Shelly said, we weren't intending to capture that activity. This technology is brand new."

"Brain scans on our workers," Bosch repeated. "Without their knowledge or consent? Oh, that's terrific." He glanced at his associates. "We'll be sued into oblivion. This is just fucking grand."

Wiggs's voice remained even. "Not a concern. The instruments have all been recalibrated. The measurements were an anomaly. They're not happening anymore. Furthermore, no one outside of this room is even aware the data exists. Happy Valley has no exposure here."

Bosch settled back in his seat. "So you set up scanners to measure the beef and ended up measuring the people, too. And?"

"And," said Wiggs, flipping to a new slide, a graph

showing two intertwining wave patterns, "remarkably, anxiety among your workers has risen in tandem with the animals, right from the start of the study. The parallels are … surprising."

Underwood stirred uneasily. "You're saying workers on our line are more stressed than they were three months ago?"

Johnson nodded. "That's correct. Stressed to the point of dysfunction. Not that you would necessarily be aware of it yet."

"Why?" asked Bosch. "What would account for that?"

"The most logical answer is that something significant in your production process has changed," said Wiggs. "That something in the way the animals and workers move or interact is different than it was three months ago."

Wiggs hesitated, then continued tentatively. "It *could* have to do with the accelerated kill speed. The shift from a knock every fifteen seconds to every twelve happened at just about the same time …"

"Don't go there," said Bosch. "We've had speed increases in the past with no negative consequences whatsoever. Kill rate's not the problem. Has to be something else."

Wiggs nodded and cleared his throat. "Understood. So at this point, we're still investigating. Analyzing the data. We don't have any definitive answers—not yet."

Bosch's eyes narrowed. "Then why are we meeting? You guys are supposed to fix problems, not just present them."

"Because of the pattern," said Wiggs, scrolling back to the slide showing the intertwining brainwave data. "The final readings from a couple days ago—before we recalibrated the scanners—showed stress and anxiety levels among your workers approaching crisis levels. In the 'red zone,' so to speak."

Bosch made no reply. Just stared at the screen.

"Based purely on the scans," said Wiggs, "your production floor is a powder keg. Ready to explode."

Another silence, and then Bosch snorted. "Either that or this whole thing is a crock of shit."

Wiggs smiled perfunctorily. "In any case," he said, "we felt it was our duty to share our findings."

****

The consultants departed, and Bosch and his subordinates sat for a while in silence. Finally, Bosch stood and exited the room. Underwood and McKenna followed.

The men made their way down a long corridor and through a series of double doors. Carpeting gave way to bare cement. Another set of double doors and now a rush of sound ahead. The rumble and whine of machines. The stench of thousands of animals jammed together—of urine and feces, fear and death. A modern American slaughterhouse operating full tilt.

They climbed metal stairs to a glassed-in viewing room high above the kill floor, and Bosch shut the door. Even through the triple-thick glass, they could hear the intermittent "thunk" of the knocker followed by a steam engine-like hiss as the captive bolt steel gun reset, followed by the boom of a 1,300-pound cow crashing onto the conveyer belt. *Thunk-hiss-boom. Thunk-hiss-boom. Thunk-hiss-boom.* Over and over again, every twelve seconds.

The men stepped to the glass and surveyed the

operation below. The cavernous kill floor looked the same as ever—at least superficially. The choreography hadn't changed. Cows entering from outside were shunted into one of six holding pens containing twenty animals each, give or take. The animals moved next to the crowd pen, where they jostled flank-to-flank in ankle-deep mud, feces, and vomit until it was time to enter the serpentine. Single file, they shuffled down the narrow high-walled lane and around three blind corners before finally emerging at the entrance to the knocking box.

The design of the serpentine was wholly intentional—to keep the animals from panicking and to keep the knocker separate from the other workers on the kill floor. To isolate and contain the act of killing.

The executives stared at the kill floor, at the rhythmic, clockwork-like movement of beasts and humans. Mist curled from vents in the floor and walls. Workers with hoses blasted the cement pathways between the pens, corralling the shit, driving it into enormous floor drains and generating billowing clouds of vapor.

Around the knocking box, the vapor was red.

"Think Wiggs is padding his hours with this scanning stuff?" Underwood asked.

Bosch shook his head. "Not Wiggs. The guy has a sterling reputation. I trust him implicitly. If he's concerned about the floor and the mental state of our workers, then I'm concerned."

Underwood and McKenna looked at each other. Baffled.

"What?" asked Bosch.

Underwood said, "I mean, you leaned on those

guys pretty hard in the meeting just now. I thought you were irritated with them."

Bosch grabbed a pair of binoculars from a shelf and began scanning the space below. "That's how you deal with vendors. Keep 'em on edge. On their toes. Stop 'em from trying to negotiate a higher price."

Underwood nodded slowly.

"Criticize and question always," Bosch continued. "Compliment and commend rarely." He shrugged. "Works with employees. Works with contractors. Works with the wife and kids, for that matter."

Underwood and McKenna laughed.

Bosch took his time surveying the floor, panning the binoculars slowly from right to left, from the spot where the animals entered the building to just beyond the knocking box—the limit of his field of view. The workers were all dressed alike—rubber boots, plastic coveralls, heavy latex gloves, hard hats, safety glasses. The supervisors wore white hard hats. The line workers, yellow. From high overhead, that was the only way to tell them apart.

Bosch looked at the workers one by one, lingering on some, adjusting the focus. Moving quickly past others. There were 120 distinct jobs on the floor, and the vast majority were held by immigrants from Mexico, Central and South America, East Africa, and Southeast Asia. The jobs were dirty, dangerous, and physically demanding. There were always tensions— based on race, gender, and job responsibilities—but Wiggs's presentation had hinted at a new level of strain.

Your production floor is a powder keg. Ready to explode.

Bosch thought about it. Considered Wiggs's

argument that the increased kill speed might be to blame and rejected the idea a split second later. Even if he believed Wiggs was right, questioning the kill speed was a non-starter. There was no slowing the line. Not now. Not ever.

Bosch's superiors—the owners, the board, the shareholders—cared first and foremost about profit. Processing more animals more quickly was the path to increased profit and a higher share price. It was Bosch's job to keep the line functioning, day and night, night and day, 24/7/365. To suggest taking a break or slowing things down would be career suicide.

A thin wire of anxiety curled in Bosch's gut. *Can't be the line speed. The crew adapted to the new speed just fine. No problems at all.*

He tasted acid in his throat. *No problems at all— except for the two fatalities the day we implemented the new routine. Who the fuck am I kidding?*

Bosch waited for his blood pressure to settle down. Truth was, the floor *had* adjusted to the new pace. There had been no further accidents or injuries since the initial mishaps. No problems at all, as far as Bosch knew, for several weeks. Things were running smoothly. And yet …

Your production floor is a powder keg.

So what's causing it? If it's not a process aberration or traffic flow issue, it has to be something else.

Bosch continued scanning. Thinking.

Not a design or flow problem. Not a mechanical issue.

Another possibility crossed his mind.

What if the malaise is man-made?

What if a person is causing it?
An individual.
A worker.

Bosch mulled the idea, analyzed it, and the rightness of the notion settled in his gut.

Worker ... or workers? In Bosch's experience, one troublemaker—one bad egg—could taint an entire group. It was true for military units. Sports teams. Corporate boards. It had to be true for the kill floor, as well.

One worker.

Bosch's anger intensified.

"Any discipline issues on the line lately?" Bosch asked without taking his eyes off the floor.

Underwood and McKenna looked at each other. "Nothing that stands out," McKenna replied. "Nothing noteworthy."

Bosch's gaze drifted to the terminus of the serpentine. To the knocking box.

The steel gate slid open, and a cow tottered forward, out of the chute and into the box. Its fur was wet and matted, its enormous brown eyes preternaturally wide.

Bosch watched the knocker swing the heavy stunning unit into position against the animal's forehead.

Thunk. Hiss. Boom.

The cow crashed to the earth, and the conveyer rumbled forward.

Practiced hands shackled the cow's hind legs, and the massive beast levitated skyward, onto the overhead line. Bosch watched the pre-sticker sever the cow's carotid artery, and the sticker slice through the jugular vein. The cow—jerking and shuddering—traveled through a ninety-degree turn and out of Bosch's field of view.

Bosch swung the binoculars back to the knocking box and focused on the knocker's face.

The man was talking.

Bosch stared.

No mistaking it. The guy was saying something. But to whom? There was no one else around.

Thunk. Hiss. Boom.

Another cow collapsed onto the conveyer, and another entered the box. The knocker swung the stunning unit into position between the beast's eyes, shut his own eyes, said something—four or five words—and fired the bolt into the animal's brain.

Thunk. Hiss. Boom.

Bosch watched the ritual play out again.

And again.

And again. Every twelve seconds.

Thunk. Hiss. Boom.

Dead meat out. Live meat in. Stunning unit up. Words spoken. A phrase. Precisely the same phrase, over and over.

Thunk. Hiss. Boom.

Bosch handed the binoculars to Underwood. "The knocker—can you tell what he's saying?"

"He sayin' something?" Underwood asked, bringing the lenses to his eyes. "To who?"

"The beef, I think."

Underwood and McKenna laughed. Bosch did not.

Underwood stared at the knocker, fine-tuning the focus. McKenna walked to a desk at the back of the room and sat down at a computer.

"Is the first word 'dozen'?" Underwood asked after a while. "It looks like he's saying 'dozen-something.'"

Bosch made no reply. Just stared through the glass, thinking. "I think it's 'cousin,'" he said finally.

"Cousin," Underwood repeated. He watched the knocker for three more minutes, time enough to witness fifteen kills and fifteen utterings. Statements. Chants— whatever they were.

"'Cousin,'" Underwood said at last. "'Please forgive us.'"

"Fuck," Bosch sighed. "That's what I think, too."

"'Cousin, please forgive us,'" Underwood repeated. "He's saying that to the cows?"

"Apparently."

McKenna called from the desk at the back of the room. "The knocker on this shift is a kid named Devon Shine. Excellent performance reviews. No discipline issues. Looks like he was offered a supervisory role in July but opted to stay on the line. Asked to work the box, specifically."

"I bet he did," said Bosch, a sudden edge to his voice. "He's a mole. Some kind of extremist. Probably working on a film."

Like every slaughterhouse owner and executive, Bosch was well aware of the threat posed by undercover animal rights activists. Infiltrators at other facilities had produced damaging exposés on everything from food safety to animal cruelty, prompting investigations and, in some cases, huge fines.

"His file is clean," said McKenna. "No criminal record. No drug issues. He graduated high school but never went to college."

"His file is probably bullshit," said Bosch.

"You want us to pull him off the line?" Underwood asked. "Fire him?"

"No," said Bosch. "Leave him right where is. For now." He looked at his men. "And not a word of this to anyone. Not a breath. Until we investigate."

McKenna and Underwood nodded but said nothing.

Bosch stared through the glass. Jaw set. A vein in his neck pulsing like a silent alarm. "He asked to work the box. No one *asks* to work the box unless they're fucked up. And he's praying with the beef. Or *to* the beef. My gut is that he's an activist, some kind of nut-job animal-rights whacko. Stirring up the crew behind the scenes. In the break room. After hours."

Bosch took the binoculars from Underwood and focused on the knocker one last time. "An employee like Mr. Shine," Bosch said, "if that's even his real name, is like a tumor. A tumor that spreads and grows and affects everything around it. We need to cut the tumor out, but we need to know how much it's metastasized first."

****

One week later

"Why did you lie on your application?" Bosch asked.

"I didn't lie," Devon Shine replied softly.

They were sitting in a sterile, windowless office with the door closed. Bosch, Underwood, and McKenna on one side of a battered metal desk. Twenty-six-year-old Devon Shine on the other. Shine had dark, wavy hair and intelligent green eyes. He was wearing street clothes. Jeans and a black T-shirt. He looked relaxed—not what Bosch had expected.

Bosch glanced at the open folder in his hand. "A Master's Degree in Animal Behavior and Bio-Ethics? Nothing about that in your application."

The young man shrugged. "The degree seemed irrelevant to an entry level position on the kill floor."

"Three-point-nine grade point average, academic honors," Bosch continued. "Impressive."

"Thanks."

"Who are you working for, Mr. Shine?"

Shine looked confused. "You," he replied. "Happy Valley Farms."

"Don't fucking play games with me, kiddo. What *group* are you with? PETA? The Humane Society? Bovine Liberation Front?"

McKenna and Underwood laughed.

"Or is this a union thing?" said Bosch. "Come in all quiet-like, under the radar, make friends, start organizing folks on the sly. Are you an organizer, Shine?"

"I don't work for any groups," said Shine. "Or unions. Nor am I a member of any."

Bosch leaned back in his chair and sighed. "You have a master's degree."

"Yes."

"And student loans?"

Shine shrugged. "A few."

Bosch tugged a sheet of paper from the folder. "A few? More like a shit-pile, I'd say. An 85,000-dollar tall shit-pile. Am I right?"

Underwood whistled under his breath.

"My goodness, son," said Bosch. "You'll be whittling away on that debt until you're ninety-two with the wages we pay here."

Shine laughed like he was embarrassed but looked straight at Bosch. "I didn't realize my finances were public record. Did you guys find that information in my locker or when you searched my apartment?"

McKenna and Underwood exchanged the briefest of glances before looking away, doing their best to appear surprised.

Bosch never blinked, but inside he was seething. The searches were supposed to have been secret. Surreptitious. He wanted to yell at his men but kept his composure. He'd deal with them later. "I don't know what you're talking about," he said to Shine. "But I assure you, I have no compunction about digging into an employee's background when I perceive a threat to this company."

A smile flickered on Shine's face. "You think I'm a threat?" he said quietly.

"I *know* you are. I'm just trying to get my brain around how big of a threat you represent. And how much damage you've already done."

"And you think this, why?" asked Shine. "Because I left my degree off my application?"

"That's part of it," said Bosch. "No one with your credentials works the kill floor. Why the hell would they?" He took another paper from the file. Glanced at it. "But according to HR, you practically begged to get in here. Emails. Phone calls. And after you *did* get hired? Wasn't two days before you started jockeying for a turn in the box."

Bosch glared at the young man. "No one with your background works the kill floor. And no one asks to work the box, *period*. No one in his right mind. We have to *assign* people to the box."

Shine said nothing.

"Then there's the bullshit chanting thing you do—whatever you call it. 'Cousin, please forgive us.' Do I have that right?"

Shine made no reply.

"Animal rights crap if I ever heard it. 'Cousin, please forgive us'? The only thing I don't know is what group you're with and what kind of sabotage or exposé you have in mind." Bosch leaned forward. Jabbed the air with one finger. "But I assure you, son, I *will* get to the bottom of it. And I won't hesitate to press charges. Criminal charges, if they're warranted. Getting fired's the least of your worries."

Shine remained quiet for a long time, his face unreadable. The room fell silent except for the murmur of conversation from somewhere in the outer office. "There *is* a threat to this company," he said at last. "To others as well. A very serious threat. But it's not me you need to worry about. I came here to help."

Bosch raised an eyebrow. "Is that a fact? So just who *should* we be worried about, Shine?"

Shine spread his hands on the table, and his youthful face looked suddenly troubled. Careworn.

"The system is broken," he said softly. "Out of whack. Unsustainable."

"What system is that?"

"The whole thing. Start to finish." Shine searched the men's faces. Saw only blank stares. He went quiet again, and his gaze fell to the desk. To his hands. When he spoke once more, his voice sounded remote. Fragile. "I've always noticed things. Even when I was a child, I saw things other people missed. Felt things other people couldn't feel."

Bosch glanced at his subordinates and wondered how long he should allow Shine to ramble. *He's playing with us. Wasting our time.* Then another thought crossed Bosch's mind. *Maybe he's genuinely fucked up. Sick in the head.* Out of morbid curiosity, he let Shine continue.

"Is that right? What kinds of things could you feel?"

"Pain," Shine replied, lifting his eyes. "Grief. Sadness. Especially with animals. I have a gift for reading animals. Understanding them. My mom called it a gift." He smiled wistfully. "Sometimes I think it's a curse."

"You feel their pain," said Bosch, a trace of a smirk in his voice. "Is that it?"

Shine registered the insult but continued in the same earnest tone. "Some feelings … some emotions … they don't dissipate on their own. They collect, you know? Fester. Build and build until …" his voice trailed off. "That's what's happening here."

Shine looked at the men, such torment in his expression that even Bosch momentarily suspended his cynicism. "I sensed this place from far away. Smelled it. Tasted it. There's a righteous rage here, Mr. Bosch. A storm of hatred and hurt darker than any funnel cloud. It's here. On top of us. Around us. And it's not going away unless things change. Unless the line changes. Unless we make amends.

"That's what I was attempting to do in the box. A little salve on the wound. A stop-gap until I could work my way into the company and explain things to people like you—to my bosses—make them see what's happening."

Crazy. Whacko. Relief swept over him. *The kid is not a mole. Not a plant. Not an undercover journalist or filmmaker. He's just bonkers. Needs professional help—big time. Fire him now and get back to work. Get on with the day.*

But Shine wasn't finished. "You may not feel things like I do," he said. "But you know there's a problem." He looked at his companions, one by one. "The escapes. The two fatalities. The results of those brain scans. You know things are amiss."

Bosch stared at Shine. Speechless. Apoplectic. Everyone knew about the escaped cows—the escapes had made the evening news. But the fatalities? The brain scans? Bosch had believed those things were secret. Buried. Hidden. Nothing close to common knowledge.

This kid will sink my career. Maybe the entire company. How does he know this shit?

Bosch's mind jumped to the fatalities. Two undocumented workers had died the day the line speed increased. One worker in the knocking box while struggling to clear a jam in the stunning unit—the unit had misfired, sending a bolt into his brain—and the other, run over by a forklift racing to move a downer cow out of the serpentine.

Bosch—under orders to keep the line going full speed no matter what—had successfully squelched both incidents by quickly settling with the victims' families and keeping the tragedies out of the news.

Bosch looked at Shine and had the unnerving feeling the kid was reading his mind. "I don't know what you think you heard," said Bosch. "In the break room or whatnot, but …"

"You think the two workers who died are gone?" Shine asked, raw pain in his voice. "They're not. You think the million or so animals we've slaughtered this year are no longer our concern? They are."

Shine gestured in the direction of the kill floor. "If you shut down the floor today, right now, the stench wouldn't just disappear. It would still reek for months. Maybe years, right? It's the same with these emotions. The rage that's collected here—*is* collecting here— won't simply evaporate. Not now. Not anymore. Not after what's happened. We're past the tipping point. The needle is in the red.

"Sadness, desolation, unspeakable suffering— human and animal—is swirling in the same pot, mixing. Making something new. Turning into something …" Shine's voice trailed away. He looked at the men, pleading. "We have to act," he said softly. "Before it's too late. We have to make amends."

Bosch stared at Shine, saying nothing—offering no rebuttal or reply—struggling to comprehend how a low-wage line employee could know the secrets he'd divulged. What it meant for the company. For him.

McKenna and Underwood asked Shine more questions. Shine responded. Bosch zoned out, lost in his own swirl of anxious thought, but he caught snippets of the conversation.

McKenna told Shine he wasn't the first animal rights activist they'd seen. Shine replied that he wasn't an animal rights activist at all. That he ate meat. That he hunted. That he thought it was okay because humans had been eating meat for millions of years.

"We're predators," said Shine. "We know that. And the animals on the line? They know they're prey.

It's the *way* it's being done that's messed up. Forcing them to live their whole lives in little boxes, pumping them full of drugs to make them grow faster, treating them like inanimate assembly line parts instead of like the sentient creatures they truly are.

"Where's the compassion?" Shine asked. "The respect? We need to slow down. Take a step back."

Bosch watched the young man, aware that his subordinates, in turn, were observing him, waiting for him to speak, to render some kind of verdict. A tiny part of Irvin Bosch was finding truth in Shine's words. But his sense of self-preservation and corporate allegiance was far stronger. *He knows things that could shut down the line. Cost me my job. Maybe send me to jail.*

Bosch settled back in his seat and smiled at the young man. "Devon," he said cheerfully, "I think I misjudged you, and I'm sorry. I'm beginning to get the picture that you really do want to help. That you sincerely want to play a role in the future of Happy Valley Farms."

McKenna and Underwood looked at Bosch in surprise, but Shine showed no reaction.

"I have to confess," Bosch continued, "I don't agree with everything you're saying, but I think you're making some important points, and I'd like to continue this conversation."

Shine made no reply.

"Go work your shift, and let's meet again tomorrow. Same time, same place. Sound okay to you?"

"Sure," said Shine, his face inscrutable.

The men shook hands at the door, and Shine

looked at Bosch. Unblinking. Unsmiling. "I believe," he said softly, "that you *will* come to see things differently …"

Bosch offered a small, tight smile.

"… that you will come to personally understand the depth and breadth of the pain this slaughterhouse and others like it are causing."

"Thank you," Bosch replied, not knowing what else to say. He watched Shine walk away, believing that things were under control and well in hand, while deep down doubting the notion at the same time.

****

Shine finished his shift and departed the kill floor the same way he always did, via the heavy steel door at the northwestern corner of the massive building. He scanned his ID badge and stepped outside. The sun had set and it was nearly dark, save for a thin ribbon of copper-colored sky on the western horizon.

Shine stood for a moment, breathing in the evening air. It felt cool and quiet outside after the heat and cacophony of the kill floor.

He started toward the employee parking lot—a vast sea of cars in the distance—and sensed movement in the shadows to his left.

A man was emerging from a weedy, litter-strewn alley between the slaughterhouse buildings, stepping over long-abandoned railroad tracks as he approached. Shine caught the glint of a car tucked in the gloom behind the man.

"Devon Shine?" said the man, coming forward. "I'm Nate Reed. Mr. Bosch sent me to pick you up. He'd like to meet for a few minutes. Now, if you're available." The man was clean-cut. Tall. Wearing a tie.

He was smiling.

Shine paused. "I'm heading home," he said. "I need a shower."

The man smiled again. "Mr. Bosch asked me to apologize for the inconvenience and said that what he has to tell you won't take more than five minutes. Also—I can give you a lift straight to your car afterward."

Shine shrugged. "Fine."

They walked toward the man's car together, navigating the uneven ground. As they got close, Shine found himself slightly in the lead. He heard a faint rustling and froze. Took a breath.

"You don't have to do this," he said, without turning. Without looking back. The man was directly behind him now.

"Just gonna give you a quick lift over to Mr. Bosch's office," said the man, the same smile in his voice.

"I can help. I want to help. If I die, I just become part of the problem."

The man pressed the silenced handgun against the back of Shine's head and fired two quick shots. *Snap, snap.*

Shine fell to the ground. The man popped open the trunk and, grunting under the weight, hefted the young man's inert body inside.

As the car pulled away, mist from Shine's brain drifted in the cool darkness—toward the vast exterior wall of the kill floor, toward intake vents with blades the size of airplane propellers spinning slowly.

****

Two weeks later

40

Happy Valley CEO Dwight Biggins rarely visited the kill floor, but he was onsite now, leading a VIP tour of board members and shareholders on break from the annual shareholder meeting at the conference center across town.

Bosch was there. He didn't have a choice. All top executives and department heads were expected to be on hand for the meet and greet. Required duty. Part of the job.

The CEO paused near the start of the serpentine and addressed the crowd, straining to be heard over the rumble and roar of the line. The throng of visitors huddled close, moving awkwardly in their spotless plastic coveralls, shiny new hard hats, and safety glasses—clutching water bottles bearing the Happy Valley Farms logo.

Bosch wondered what the workers thought of the visiting dignitaries—a group of mostly white, mostly male executives smiling and laughing and snapping pictures with their smart phones. Bosch couldn't wait for them to leave.

The CEO droned on. Bosch looked around. Ever since his run-in with Shine, things on the line had been calm. Calmer than normal. No fights. No breakdowns— no berserk or downer cows to impede production.

Bosch was not reassured. The little voice in his head told him that the calm on the kill floor was the calm before the storm.

Your production floor is a powder keg. Ready to explode.

The CEO was practically yelling now, bragging about Happy Valley delivering more product today than at any time in company history.

Then the power died.

Machines stopped. Lights went out. The line fell silent. Workers and VIPs gawked, turning this way and that. Cows mooed and shuffled and groaned.

Sunlight filtering through upper-story windows and skylights made the vast gray room feel somehow even larger, like a desolate ruin in a forgotten civilization.

"Backup generators should kick on here in a second," the CEO said glibly.

They didn't.

The light diminished even further—as if there'd been a sudden, total eclipse of the sun—and the production floor vanished in a smothering darkness.

"What's going on?" cried one of the VIPs.

"What happened to the light?"

Bosch's heart hammered, and he swayed in the blackness, ready to bolt. Ready to scream.

Shine's here. This is Shine's doing. We're going to die.

The lights blinked back on, and the CEO laughed. The assembly line coughed to life, and the workers looked around. Looked at each other.

Bosch breathed, and his whole body relaxed. *A simple power outage. Nothing more. What a pussy I am.*

"Never a dull moment here at Happy Valley Farms," joked the CEO. "Not sure what that was about, but it looks like we're back on track."

Amid the lighthearted banter, the CEO caught Bosch's eye fleetingly and fixed him with a *what the fuck?* look acid enough to dissolve steel.

Bosch imagined the questions to come. The blame. The finger-pointing. He figured the outage might even cost him his job. He didn't care. He was just glad to be alive.

****

The VIP entourage migrated outside, to *Receiving*—a broad, manure-packed yard with multiple steel gangways along one fence jutting skyward like imbalanced teeter-totters.

Cattle trucks approaching the yard could pull tight against the gangways and release their hoofed cargo from the side. Most of the trucks that served Happy Valley Farms had two lateral doors for quicker unloading. Some had three.

Receiving could accommodate several trucks at a time, but there was only one in the yard now—a giant, mud-caked semi actively disgorging a flood of stumbling, decrepit-looking dairy cows.

Standing in the middle of the yard, the CEO conferred briefly with a supervisor, then turned, smiling, to the VIPs.

"And these," he said, with a sweep of his arm, "are four-year-olds from our Milton Creek Dairy operation."

He chuckled as the beasts funneled past, toward the entrance to the kill floor. "Four years of constant impregnation and milk production and these gals are ready for retirement."

Laughter all around.

Laughter. Then, silence.

Stillness.

Quiet.

Bosch stared. The VIPs stared back. The CEO's mouth was open, but no sound was coming out.

Bosch wondered what the hell they were all doing—pretending to be frozen like that. Immobile. Unmoving. Like department store mannequins.

They looked comical. Choreographed. A farmyard flash mob.

That's when Bosch realized he was frozen, too.

Frozen. Paralyzed. Bolted to the ground. Unable to twist or turn. His eyes still worked, though. He could still see. And what he saw in his companions' eyes was shock, turning to panic.

Bosch gawked, and the horizon behind the VIPs rolled.

Then he was falling, spinning.

Nausea twisted his insides.

Bosch shut his eyes, but the spinning continued for a long time.

At last, the movement slowed. Stabilized.

Bosch opened his eyes and discovered that he was closer to the ground. *Am I stooping? Did I fall down?* He couldn't remember, and he couldn't tell.

He was looking in a different direction now. That was clear. Staring at the backside of a dairy cow.

Bosch moved again—at last. Lifted his right leg, took a step, put it down.

He caught sight of the leg and shivered. Then he lifted the appendage again and examined it.

This is my leg.

A cow's leg.

Once more, he lurched lazily, painfully forward, and fresh understanding blossomed in his brain— inevitable and incontrovertible.

We've traded places—the animals and the people.

He took another faltering step and felt the full heaviness and decrepitude of his bovine frame. His new body was unwell. In agonizing pain.

He recalled Shine's words. *"I believe that you will*

come to see things differently ... to personally understand the depth and breadth of the pain this slaughterhouse and others like it are causing."

Bosch looked around and saw that all of the VIPs and Happy Valley executives now inhabited bovine bodies. The eyes gave it away. The eyes told the story—flashes of human emotion and intelligence flickering inside those sad brown orbs.

Wet and wide with terror, the eyes darted this way and that—seeking an end to the joke. The nightmare.

Bosch recognized the CEO in one set of eyes. Even imprisoned inside a sagging dairy cow, the man's pompous persona cut through. There was fury and indignation in those eyes. A look that thundered, *Just wait until I get this nonsense sorted out! Heads will roll!*

The CEO cow tried to break away from the herd. Others did, as well. But the wranglers were having none of it. They had no inkling of the transmogrification that had just occurred and assumed that the cows were just being unruly. That something had upset them.

Calling to one another in Spanish, deploying cattle prods and whips, the wranglers corralled the beasts and drove them forward toward the open doors of the kill floor.

Bosch fought back, like the rest—to no avail. His body was too weak. Too battered and depleted. The best he could manage was to twist his bovine head one final time—long enough to see what had become of his old body and the bodies of the other VIPs.

He stared.

The people—if that's what they still were—were moving away, toward the road, walking stiffly, jerkily—like automatons. Zombies.

Bosch wondered what was driving his old body since he was no longer at the helm. Then he understood. Somehow, he knew.

It was Shine. Shine and all the rest. The dead workers. The dead animals. A mélange of mental energy—an ocean of rage and pain—finding an outlet at last, manifesting, seizing an opportunity. Setting off to put things right.

Shine had wanted to change the system from the inside. Robbed of that opportunity and of his life, he had found another way.

Bosch felt the awful sting of a wrangler's whip and turned back to see that the entrance to the kill floor was much closer now.

The doors were open. Darkness beyond. It struck Bosch then that the doors resembled a mouth. The gaping, voracious maw of a demon.

Liam Teller

Wanderings

I sat in the deepest, darkest part of the old forest—angry, bitter, and alone.

I couldn't have put it into words at age twelve, but I *needed* to be alone. To spend the entire day deep in the trees, thinking, remembering, and saying goodbye.

Mom knew where I was and what I was feeling. Looking back on it, I realize my parents were as upset by the whole situation as I was. They were just processing things differently. Grieving differently. They were adults. I was a kid.

I wanted solitude. But that's not what I found.

The boy emerged from the woods with barely a rustle. In fact, I didn't even notice him at first.

A stirring of the air caused me to lift my eyes. Or perhaps I smelled him. Judging from his appearance, he hadn't bathed in months.

The hairs on the back of my neck prickled. He stood watching me. A slender reed of a boy. Barefoot. Black eyes, wide and staring. A blank, slack-jawed expression. Mouth a flaccid oval.

I sensed immediately that there was something wrong with him. On a different day, in a different environment, I might have shown compassion and kindness, but I was not in the mood to be kind.

"What do you want?" I said.

He tipped his head, blinking stupidly. "You sad." It was a statement, not a question.

I laughed bitterly. "No. I'm fucking overjoyed.

Can't you tell?"

I rarely used profanity. It certainly was not allowed in my house. And the f-word felt forced and awkward as it passed my lips. But it was also somehow soothing. As if I'd just freed some of my rage.

"Well, you *look* sad," he said, missing my sarcasm entirely.

Something wrong with him. Special needs.

And clearly his shortcomings went beyond mental impairment. Now that I had a better look, that was plain enough. Shoeless and dressed in grungy, threadbare denim overalls and a tan shirt made of some kind of stiff canvas, he looked like no one I'd ever seen on the island before. If his clothes were a joke, his hair was even more shocking: a matted tangle of greasy black mixed with inexplicable streaks of white. Oily strands fell into his eyes, and he reflexively pushed them away. He looked like a character from a movie about the Depression or Dust Bowl.

I resisted the urge to ask questions. I wanted to be alone. Wanted the weird kid to go away.

He didn't budge. "Why you pining so?"

Pining so?

"Where the hell are you from?" I asked. I wouldn't even have known what "pining" meant if I hadn't just read *Old Yeller* in Ms. Mirandez's class.

He gave no reply. Just stared. I stared back, saying nothing. The last thing I wanted was a dialogue with this imbecile. He was ruining what I had envisioned as a sacred day. This part of the forest was, in a very real sense, my church, and he was crashing my service. Wrecking everything.

"Why you pining so?" I said, imitating his nasal

voice. "Are you a fucking idiot?" The f-word came more easily this time. "Don't you know what's happening? What the hell's wrong with you?"

The strange boy made no reply. Just cocked his head to the other side, as if the new angle would give him a different perspective on things. I shivered, and gooseflesh rippled on my arms. More was off about this kid than his appearance. No doubt about that.

I ignored my alarm. Buried it in anger and frustration. "They're killing this place tomorrow," I said, practically spitting the words. "Which you would know already if you weren't a total idiot. Cutting all the trees. Bulldozing everything. Carving roads. Digging trenches. Destroying the whole three hundred seven acres. For houses. A mini-mart. *'Why you pining so?'* Everyone should be 'pining,' you moron."

The boy looked around, wide-eyed. If my insults had angered him, he didn't show it. "The whole thing?"

"Every last leaf and twig." This wasn't literally true. After multiple lawsuits and negotiations with the City of Bainbridge Island, the developer had agreed to leave a seven-foot-wide "buffer zone" along the stream and maintain a fern garden in the center of the development. To me and many other people, the concessions seemed more an insult than a solution to anything. Razing a one hundred fifty-year-old forest but leaving a tiny buffer zone and patch of ferns, which would very likely die without the surrounding rain forest, seemed like a cruel joke. A begrudging, mocking morsel of appeasement tossed out to an angry public based on the advice of some big city attorney.

My fury resurged after I thought about the buffer and what would become of my beloved stream, with its quiet pools, cattails, and iridescent butterflies.

"Haven't you seen the orange tape? All the machines?" I waved in the direction of a gravel staging area a few hundred yards to the east. The space was packed with equipment. Treaded bulldozers, backhoes, dump trucks. The staging area contained a mobile home on blocks, too, which, according to my dad, the construction company would use as an office and headquarters. There was security as well. The protests had been so fierce, the fight so bitter, that the developers weren't taking any chances. Armed men guarded the machines 24/7. I hated them all.

My dad had told me not to blame the workers and security guys. "They're just trying to feed their families," he said. "This isn't their fault. If you want to blame someone, blame the city council. Blame the developers. Blame human greed."

This completely logical exhortation did not pacify my hot-blooded, twelve-year-old, budding environmentalist's brain. All I knew was that I loved the forest, and it was about to die.

My forest. That's how I thought of it. Source of a thousand adventures. Countless games of army and hide-and-seek with my friends. Font of magic and mystery, it fed my soul. I would never have phrased it so at the time, but it's true. To destroy such a place was a monstrous violation. Like murder.

The boy looked around again, taking his time, then flicked his gaze back to me. "Whatcha gonna do about it?"

I snorted, startled by the profound, unvarnished ignorance of the question. "Do? There's nothing anyone can do. We tried. We fought. We lost. It's too late."

"Ain't really too late."

This pissed me off all over again. "You don't know what the hell you're talking about," I said, the words catching in my throat. "This was a battle. And we lost. Tons of people fought this in court—my family included. People wrote a million letters. My friends and me and tons of other kids marched. Went door to door. We tried everything. But we lost. And all this is going away tomorrow."

The boy appeared to suddenly lose interest in the conversation. He turned to the stream, dropped to his knees next to the deepest pool, and cast about until he found a stick. Then he scooched forward on his belly until his head was protruding over the lip of the pool and began dabbing at the water with the stick.

I stared at his prone form. His feet were so calloused and caked with dirt that I wondered if he had ever worn shoes. The denim of his overalls, barely recognizable as denim, was thin and tattered, with more patched areas than unpatched ones.

He poked at the water, singing softly to himself. I could not discern the words, though the tune sounded vaguely familiar. He seemed to have forgotten all about me.

Like it or not, I was now consumed with curiosity. This was not at all how I had envisioned my day unfolding. My attention was on this freaky little kid. Not where I wanted it to be.

I looked beyond the boy, wondering where he lived. He'd emerged from the deepest, wildest part of the grove. Two hundred unbroken acres of old trees and dense undergrowth. No trails that way—too boggy and brambly.

A ruin of sorts sat a few hundred yards in, on the hillside. The barest remnants of a long-forgotten town that existed briefly in the 1860s, when Blakely Harbor was home to the world's largest sawmill. There was nothing left of the "town" now except for a few moss-covered sections of wall here and there among the ferns.

I'd explored the ruins with my dad and friends the previous summer. We kids built up the outing in our minds—convinced we'd find a lost city, with treasure, of course, straight out of Indiana Jones. In fact, it was a big letdown. Nothing much at all to look at. Without GPS coordinates from the Bainbridge Historical Museum, we would've missed the site entirely.

The boy abruptly stopped singing. He twisted in the dirt and looked at me. "Minnow Men stop it, all right," he said.

"Minnow what?"

"Minnow Men stop it, sure enough."

I laughed. "That makes, like, zero sense."

He began dabbing at the water once more. The soft singing resumed.

I groaned, got to my feet, and crossed to stand next to him. All week, I'd been vacillating between sadness and rage. Sadness came to the fore now and I regarded the boy with sudden compassion.

He's disabled. Clearly a special needs kid. Not his fault if he doesn't understand what's going on.

It dawned on me that he might be lost. That I might need to help him find his way home.

I sat on the bank next to the boy. I'd played here—alone and with friends—countless times. The stream ran reliably year-round—a rare thing on Bainbridge.

The water flowed down from the ridge, through deep forest and fern-filled gullies, across sun-dappled meadows, and around majestic old maple trees. In most places, the stream was just a narrow cataract winding its way downhill, but in spots, there were tranquil pools full of life—minnows and frogs, salamanders and garter snakes. My friends and I had seen deer drinking from this pool. Raccoons and barred owls, even black bear occasionally visited after swimming over from the Peninsula. I'd never actually seen a bear here, but I'd seen their tracks in the mud along the bank.

A pair of purple butterflies wafted over the water, catching the morning light, and I thought again about the change the coming days would bring. Starting tomorrow, there would be noise and mayhem. The scream of saws and the smell of gasoline. Stately old trees that, I believed, possessed supernatural powers would crash to Earth.

For the moment, everything around me was still intact and functioning. The trees whispered in the breeze, oblivious to the destruction ahead. The birds, animals, and insects carried on with their busy lives.

Or maybe the forest is aware.

The idea landed abruptly in my mind with the force of a migraine. The pain passed quickly, leaving me with a weird feeling. Looking around, I thought the idea might be right. The forest was unusually still and quiet, like it was waiting for something.

I looked at the boy again, watching as he dabbed his stick randomly into the clear water, singing soft and low. Minnows jetted this way and that over clean gravel, apparently unfazed by his movements.

He's too simple to conceive of the destruction to

come. But maybe he loves the forest as much as I do. In his own way. Maybe he'll be devastated, too. Maybe it will be worse for him.

I said gently, "You think the minnows could help us save the forest? Is that what you meant a minute ago?"

He stopped singing and rose to a sitting position, his overalls mud-caked and askew on his chest. He tugged absently at his shirt sleeve, crossed his legs, and looked at me. "Minnow Men stop the things you worried about," he said softly.

"Minnow Men?" I looked at the pool. "You mean minnows?"

He frowned. "Minnow Men come up from minnows, all right. But these here is just minnows. They ain't imbued."

Imbued. I had no idea what the word meant, but my supply of compassion was running low again.

"You're talking nonsense," I said, more harshly than I intended. "Minnows can't do anything."

He nodded in agreement, his strange eyes fixed on mine. "Not like they is. Not without Shiny Black from the Void."

I laughed. But the laugh was a cover. Something in his words made me shiver. I tried to keep my voice light. "Shiny *what* from the *what?*"

"Shiny Black. From the Void."

"You're crazy."

He shrugged.

"Shiny Black from the Void will do *what* exactly?"

The boy smiled for the first time since we'd met, revealing surprisingly straight, clean teeth.

"Bring bedlam," he said.

Another chill. A surge of adrenaline. As if I'd just discovered a poisonous spider on my arm. Nothing this boy said made the slightest bit of sense. Yet something in his words struck a chord.

"You're nuts," I said. "There's no 'Void' and no 'Shiny Black.' What the hell's wrong with you?"

The boy nodded gravely. "Yes sir, Zach Nelson. There is. There's some a each under your house."

"*My* house? And wait—how do you know my name?"

"You done told it to me."

Had I told him my name? I didn't think so.

"There's nothing under my house except a crawl space full of deer mice, spiders, and old boards. And my mom's kayak."

"There's a void, all right," he said confidently. "A live one. And enough Shiny Black for what we need, sure enough."

"Did somebody hit you in the head?"

He ignored the question and peered past me—like he'd just heard someone calling his name. He looked at me again.

"Shiny Black's there, Zach Nelson. Won't last, though. Never does."

"You're full of shit."

He stared at me blankly. Not a trace of hurt or anger. Insults were useless against this kid.

I sighed, exasperated. "Fine. Let's go. I'll prove it to you."

I let the boy lead, wondering if he actually knew the way to my house. After a couple of minutes of hiking, it became clear that he did.

We crossed Old Towne Road and entered Ellington

Heights—a half-mile long, mostly wooded neighborhood of modest homes set on two and a half-acre lots. I felt suddenly self-conscious walking next to the little freak. I wondered what my friends would say if they saw us together. Now that we were out of the woods, he looked even more weird.

"What's your name," I asked.

"Liam Teller."

"Where do you live, Liam?"

He waved absently at the forest. "Back away yonder."

Yonder? Who says "yonder?"

A million questions spun in my mind. *How did he know my name? Where I live? Where had he come from?*

He seemed so harmless—this spindly-armed nothing of a boy—but there was a force or gravity about him that his meager appearance could not conceal.

I felt like I was floating in a current in a wide river. For the moment, I was still close to shore. Still safe. But the eddies were getting stronger, drawing me out and away, toward a fate I couldn't see.

Part of me wanted to abandon the strange kid, run straight to my house, and bolt the door. Another part wanted to prove to the little weirdo that there was nothing under my house. Once that happened, I reasoned, he'd go away, and I could return to my forest. Salvage the remainder of the day.

If I hide in my house now, I'll never come out, I told myself. *The destruction will start tomorrow morning, and it'll be too late. I'll lose my forest without saying goodbye.* This was unacceptable.

"There's nothing under my house," I repeated, as we topped a fern-covered hill and dropped into my backyard. I marveled at the fact that we hadn't seen another soul—child or adult—since emerging from the forest. *Strange. A summer Sunday, and no one's mowing the lawn? Washing the car? Shooting hoops?*

My house—basically a thirty by thirty wooden box set on concrete piers with wrap-around cedar decks—lay directly ahead. My folks—environmentalists from way back—had worked with an architect to minimize the impact of construction. The slope was naturally wet. And runoff from our land fed a fifteen-acre wetland farther downhill. Rather than excavate for a foundation, they'd decided on a less invasive plan—building the house just above ground on concrete piers. Ferns and rhododendrons grew right up to the edge of the deck.

"There's a void all right," said Liam Teller. "A live one."

Mere paces from the house now, I thought about all the times my friends and I had played around the edges of the crawl space.

We used to go deep underneath, until my buddy Henry Murdon got bitten by a spider, and my mom made a rule that we couldn't go in more than three feet. Still, we built forts along the edge and took advantage of the clear view to spy on approaching enemies.

Once, when I was six or seven, during the hottest part of August, a river otter crawled under the house and died. The stench was so bad, we almost had to stay in a hotel. My dad, holding a heavy-duty trash bag and wearing a headlamp, rubber gloves, and a respirator he bought at Ace, slithered into the space to retrieve the otter carcass as my little sister and I watched from way back in the yard, where the stench wasn't quite so bad. Even through the respirator, we could hear my dad's curses.

I'd mostly ignored the crawl space for the past year, as my interests transitioned away from things like army and hide-and-seek. Still, I was certain the expanse would be clear, as always. One look would confirm it. I smiled, confident that I was seconds away from shooting down Liam's strange tale and sending him on his way.

We neared the deck, and my confidence began to wane. Something was off about the scene in front of us. I couldn't have explained it then, and I can't explain it now. Superficially, all appeared normal. The house. The yard. The surrounding forest. The sparkling Sound far below. Mt. Rainier in the distance.

But something's wrong.

I wished my mom or dad or even my annoying sister would come out onto the deck, but I had the strangest feeling that they *couldn't* come out. Not now. *Not right now.*

We reached the deck, dropped to our knees, and peered under the house. My heart skipped a beat. There was something in the middle of the crawl space. Something big, blocking the light.

A tarp. That was my first thought. A simple, sensible explanation.

Dad brought home that huge tarp he uses to cover the sailboat and stuffed it under there.

"Let's go," said Liam. "Shiny Black won't last."

"It's just a tarp," I said feebly.

Liam made no reply. Just lunged forward on hands and knees.

Reluctantly I followed, crawling in most places and slithering on my belly where the trusses hung low, like a soldier sneaking into an enemy camp.

Craning my neck, I peered ahead, trying to see around Liam and get a read on what lay in the center. *A tarp, that's all it is.*

My confidence dimmed as we neared the heart of the crawl space and darkness deepened around us.

A sound triggered a fresh pulse of adrenaline. I wanted to wriggle backward in the dirt and flee. I told myself it was just a house-related noise—air flowing from a vent in the floor. But it wasn't a mechanical sound.

"Liam," I whispered. "What the hell is that?"

He ignored me. Or maybe he didn't hear the question. In any case, he kept slithering forward. I paused a moment, and Liam nearly vanished from sight. Within a second or two, only his feet were visible.

I scrambled on, afraid of losing my way.

Absurd, I told myself. *I'm under my own house.*

Thing is, it didn't feel like familiar territory. Not at all. I had a sudden, panic-inducing vision of being trapped in the darkness and dying like the otter. I pictured my parents discovering my decomposing body. I kept moving.

The air changed around us—from wet and mildewy to dry and stale. The air of a museum vault. A tomb.

And now the sound again. A low, wheezing intake of air followed by a languid exhalation. The cycle repeated, again and again. Breathing.

Gooseflesh rippled on my arms once more as I pictured an immense, slumbering body in the gloom ahead. The dry air grew frigid.

"We here," said Liam, his voice jarring and abrasive in the bone-dry air. "Hold my ankles now."

We'd crawled right to the edge of whatever was blocking the crawl space, and still I had no understanding of what "it" was. Not a tarp. Definitely not a tarp. Darkness flowed around us like water, coating the ground and ceiling, obscuring the concrete piers, swallowing the light.

I wanted so badly to retreat. To speed-crawl to the light and stand in the July sunshine. Breathe normal air. I wanted to run into my house, bolt the doors, and ask my parents to explain what I'd seen. Surely, they would have a logical explanation.

I grabbed Liam's bony ankles, and his body tensed and went rigid. I could see nothing beyond his waist. I kept thinking my eyes would adjust, but they never did.

Liam's body bent and twisted, side-to-side and up and down, the same pattern over and over again. The breathing sound continued, slow and rhythmic. It seemed to be coming from all directions.

What in the hell is happening?

And then Liam was shimmying backward and pivoting around. Breathing hard. His words came in ragged gasps. "You gotta carry some, Zach Nelson. Shiny Black all the time come up heavy." He shoved something into my hands with a grunt, and I received it, unable to make out what it was—though we were facing the light once more.

A roundish rock with a heavily pitted surface. That's what it felt like. About the size of a grapefruit or softball. "Heavy" was an understatement. It felt much heavier than a brick or similar-sized rock from the garden. Once, at a museum, I'd lifted a small cannonball. It felt like that, only heavier.

I was thinking about rolling the object in front of me. Liam Teller read my mind. "Carry it, don't let it touch the Earth none. Hold it tight."

I didn't argue. Just struggled forward, wanting to escape the crawl space.

The light spread around us, and I saw now that Liam was carrying a chunk of the same dark material, straining just as hard as me.

I powered forward, side-crawling on my left hand, holding the object tight against my ribs with my right, like a football player fighting to cross the goal line.

What happens if you drop Shiny Black? I didn't know and didn't want to find out. I had a feeling it couldn't be anything good.

I crawled on, sometimes slipping in the soft dirt, sometimes finding purchase and gaining a few inches.

After what seemed like hours, we reached the edge and daylight and struggled to our feet, straining mightily under the weight of the strange material.

I looked at Liam. His clothes were even filthier than before, if that was possible. Great cotton candy-like clots of cobweb adorned his hair.

I glanced at the substance in my hands and felt a needle-sharp pain—as if I'd inadvertently looked at the sun. The material was the opposite of bright, but it burned all the same. Obsidian-black, it seemed to swallow the light around it. In the split-second glance I could tolerate, I noticed something else. The object appeared to change—to move and writhe—as I held it.

"Don't look at it none," Liam said. "Just hold it tight now."

He squatted and peered under the house once more. "Just in time," he said.

I squatted next to him, holding the Shiny Black with both hands. The breath caught in my throat. The space under the house was clear. Empty and open, as always, nothing in the middle of the expanse except concrete piers and heavy wooden trusses.

We started our return to the forest, tottering under the weight of our burdens. I glanced back at my house, expecting to see my mom or dad on the deck, but there was no one.

Where is everyone?

I followed Liam. It seemed the only logical thing to do. Clearly, I'd misjudged the boy. The things he'd said were beyond strange, but at least some of them were true. He'd said we'd find something under my house, and we had. The substance I held in my hands was real. I had no idea what it was or what it could do, if anything, or if it was actually called "Shiny Black" by anyone but Liam Teller, but I was so intrigued that I momentarily forgot my grief.

We made it through the entire neighborhood— again—without seeing a soul. No people. No dogs. No cars. No airplanes either, now that I considered it. Empty. Quiet. Not normal. Not at all. *Is everyone inside their house, grieving the coming destruction? Unlikely.*

We plunged back into the forest, twice resting against fallen trees, sweating and gasping for breath. We didn't talk.

Back at the streamside, Liam said, "Hold this," and dropped his Shiny Black into my arms before I could object. The combined weight of the two masses was almost unbearable, and I cried out.

Liam scrambled about, ripping up handfuls of fern fronds and making a little bed on the bank of the pool.

"Liam," I said. "Hurry. I'm going to drop them." Even as I said the words I realized "them" had become one object. I couldn't understand it. The Shiny Black had seemed to me solid as any rock. And when Liam set his portion in my arms the two objects had "clunked" together like stone. Yet in my arms, they'd somehow merged into a single, immensely heavy ball.

Liam took the mass and set it carefully on the bed of ferns.

"What is that stuff?" I asked.

"Shiny Black. What we need."

A completely unsatisfying answer, but I didn't press.

Liam squatted by the pool and stared at the water.

"Now what?"

"Reflection," said Liam.

"What does that mean?"

He lay on his belly, as before, and peered into the pool. "Rest a spell," he said offhandedly. I couldn't tell if he was talking to me or the fish, but I suddenly felt very weary.

I sat in the moss and watched Liam. He found his stick and began dabbing at the water again, singing softly. After a moment, he pivoted, touched the stick to the black mass, then went back to the water.

It dawned on me that what he was doing might be bad for the minnows, that the black stone or tar or whatever it was might kill them. Then I remembered what was coming the next day and realized it really didn't matter. Most everything in the creek was going to die anyway.

I lay back and looked up into the lush, green canopy of the forest, the events of the bizarre, stressful morning swirling in my mind. The branches swayed in the breeze, whispering softly. This sound, mixed with the murmur of the creek and Liam's low, lilting song lulled me to sleep.

I awoke once—sort of. The light had changed. A lot. It was much later in the day. I knew that I should be alarmed, but I could not bring myself to rise. My limbs felt leaden. My eyes fluttered but would not stay open—no matter how much I willed them to, as if I'd been anesthetized.

Liam was singing still, I remember that. But his song had changed into something darker. More discordant. The dreams that came when I slipped back into sleep were violent. Disturbing. But I don't recall details.

I remember something else about the brief period of wakefulness—the sense that Liam knew I was awake, though his back was to me, and was holding me inert and immobile, as if he needed to finish his work without interruption.

When I awoke again, it was early evening. Sunlight filtered low through the trees. I came up onto my elbows, frightened and disoriented. I froze.

Ghost-like shapes were rising from the pool and shambling away into the forest. Climbing from the water, standing a moment, then stepping quickly on, one after another. Water dripped from glistening bodies. Errant droplets caught the light of the dying sun and shone like gold.

My somnolent brain marveled at the absurdity of the scene. The pool was tiny, just a few feet across and no more than eighteen inches deep. Yet a small army of life-sized ghost men emerged from the hole in rapid succession. Clearly, I was still asleep. Still dreaming.

I shook my head and rubbed my eyes and awoke for real.

I was alone. The forest was quiet. Liam Teller was nowhere to be seen. The black blob was gone as well. But the bed of ferns was still there. The fronds pressed flat against the earth.

I walked home in a fog, my head spinning with all that had transpired. I shared none of what had happened with my parents or sister, and the evening passed quietly.

It felt strange to be back in a house with electric lights and the noise of appliances and television.

I fell asleep thinking about Liam Teller and the strange darkness under my house and wondered if the entire day had been a dream after all. It seemed almost impossible to separate what had actually happened from things I might have imagined. I wondered if there was something wrong with me.

I awoke—my whole family, the whole neighborhood awoke—in the middle of the night to the wail of sirens and the roar of fire engines. The red and blue light of emergency flashers ricocheted off the walls of my bedroom.

I found my sister and parents standing on the deck, watching the commotion. The night air was thick with smoke. Trucks rumbled into position. Voices reverberated on loudspeakers.

Mom read from one of the island Facebook feeds. "Fire at the staging area," she said. "The police are reporting possible fatalities."

More emergency vehicles arrived, including many from off the island. It was a big fire. The possibility of fatalities meant swarms of police and emergency personnel. I don't think anyone in the Ellington Heights neighborhood slept any more that night.

****

Now, twenty years on, I've moved back to Bainbridge with my wife and two young kids, after years of college, graduate school, and career-building in faraway cities.

It's a sleepy summer Saturday when I return to the forest. My wife and kids are away for the weekend. I find the old path through the woods. The forest is still here, though much has changed. Most of the cedars are dead or dying. Many other trees as well—all from the effects of climate change. Water has become a huge issue on the island, and everything looks dry.

Like everywhere on earth, weather patterns are rapidly shifting. There never used to be ticks. Now ticks are everywhere. Lyme Disease is a big problem. Disease-carrying mosquitoes, too. The Sound still sparkles in the distance, though beneath the waves scarcely any life, aside from algae, remains.

I try to focus on the good things. The island is still the best place I've ever found. If we're heading into some kind of last stand as a species, I'm content to make it here. I look around, remembering all the times I played in these woods with my friends.

After the fire all those years ago, a massive investigation ensued. Two security guards and a construction foreman died. Autopsy reports showed they'd been bludgeoned to death before the fire began. Swarms of FBI and ATF agents descended on the site in the days following the conflagration, interviewing everyone for miles around and pursuing every possible lead. The fire and homicides made national news.

The investigation delayed the start of development for more than a year, and in the interim, the developer went broke. A conservation group raised enough money to buy the entire forest and create a memorial for the murdered men. Three years after the fire, the land officially became a three hundred seven-acre park.

The crimes were never solved. No suspects were arrested. I read recently that the investigation continues, though on a much smaller scale.

I think about all of this as I walk to my old favorite spot deep in the woods.

The stream looks the same. The pool is still here. I check, and sure enough, there are still minnows darting about in the shallows.

I sit in the moss and close my eyes. I meditate, or try to, but an old and familiar worry tugs painfully at my consciousness. *Am I in any way responsible for the deaths of those men?*

"No," is my simple, adamant response.

I tell myself now, as I have at least a thousand times before, that the notion is ridiculous. That we were just kids. That our silly make-believe game could not have caused fire and death. Always within these sensible-seeming arguments, a slender thread of doubt lingers.

I think and wonder, and when I open my eyes, Liam Teller is standing beside the pool, as I somehow knew he would be. It's ridiculous and impossible, of course, but he looks completely unchanged from the last time I saw him. I don't question that it's him. I don't wonder if it's a different boy that looks like Liam Teller. I know with dead certainty that it *is* him.

We sit together and talk. And I realize now that conversing with this boy is not like communicating with other people. Conversations with Liam Teller seem to happen in a kind of fog, separate and apart from normal reality. Inside this bubble, everything makes sense, in its own bizarre way. But once an encounter ends, trying to remember what was communicated is virtually impossible.

"You carrying a burden, Zach Nelson," Liam says, in his plain, matter-of-fact way.

I tell him I don't know what he's talking about, even though I do.

"A heavy burden, all right."

I tell Liam that I've moved back to the island and have young kids. I get the sense he already knows this. I tell him that I'm grateful the forest survived but alarmed by all the changes happening everywhere. I tell him I wish I could do something.

"But the fact is, we're too late." I say. "The planet is dying. We have too many people. Too much greed. Nothing's going to change in time. I'm sad for my kids. Sad all the time, thinking we shouldn't even have had kids because the world is dying, and there's nothing I can do about it."

Liam sits by the stream, alternately gazing at the pool and into the forest.

"Not too late, Zach Nelson," he says after a while. "Won't be easy. But it's not too late."

I say to the boy, "Tell me what we need to do."

Emily

Wanderings

I am not sure that I exist, actually.
—Jorge Luis Borges

On the broad, grassy steppe overlooking Agate Gap, high above the rusting ruins of the old trestles, sat a small, cedar-sided house, lonely and isolated.

The only thing lonelier than the house above the Gap was the little girl who lived there. Ten-year-old Abigail Barrett.

Abigail was lonely because there were no other people around. Not one.

Directly across the Gap was another patch of open ground that looked to Abigail like a mirror image of her own domain—grassy meadow backed by dark and foreboding forest. There was a house on the far steppe, as well. An identical twin of Abigail's dwelling but unoccupied.

A precarious rope bridge suspended high above the chasm provided the only link between the two homesteads, and the bridge groaned and shivered in the wind.

The land on the other side of the Gap was called Indian Heath. No one walked its trails.

As far as Abigail knew, no one lived within a thousand miles in any direction.

Of course, there *had* been other people, years earlier. Abigail could remember. But they'd all moved on, after the Breaking. She clung to vague memories of loved ones waving goodbye, melting into the fog, gliding into the forest. Long lines of ethereal beings receding into the gloom. She ached with longing whenever she looked at the forest. But she never dared go there.

Abigail was, in fact, a sort of prisoner on her broad, grassy bench, though she never would have described things that way. She was far too positive a soul for that.

Abigail thought, from time to time, about building a boat but knew she didn't have the skills. She contemplated following her long-lost community into the forest, but that way was even more frightening than the sea. The ancient road was shattered and overgrown. Shards of asphalt jutted from the undergrowth like broken teeth.

She kept an eye out for ships and sometimes thought she saw movement on the far horizon, but no vessels ever ventured close to the Gap.

And so, Abigail—being optimistic by nature—made the best of her situation. She kept very busy, caring for her small house, tending her garden, fishing, and digging for clams. And she made friends with the animals and birds that lived nearby.

She talked to the dolphins and sea otters that swam close to shore and to the seals that climbed onto the rocks below her house. She told stories to the tufted puffins, storm petrels, and double-crested cormorants that nested among the cliffs. She sang to the pigeon guillemots and black oystercatchers as they prowled the beach for tiny crabs.

Abigail gave some of her animal companions names and considered a few of them true friends. Still—being a person herself—she longed for human companionship.

A sister. That's what I want. A sister. Younger or older or exactly the same age—I don't care.

A sister to play with and talk to. To laugh and sing with. A friend to share meals and stories, sunrises and sunsets.

Just thinking about such a companion made Abigail happy, and she often found herself daydreaming.

Her name would be Emily. My sister. Emily.

Abigail's memories of the people who had once lived with her were dim and dream-like. She had been very young then, barely aware of the world. Still, she remembered a few things—such as how good it felt to have other special people close by.

She remembered kind voices and warm laughter, smiling faces, and eyes full of love and compassion. She remembered sitting with others on the beach on calm nights, when moonlight reflected off the tranquil sea, and staring into a bonfire as voices rang in the darkness.

And she remembered the Breaking, as the land split with a noise like thunder and lightning shattered the darkness. She remembered the sea, rising like a wall, then falling away again, and sudden, searing heat followed by months of soothing rain. She remembered the lonesome whine of the wind.

Such thoughts swirled in Abigail's mind as she went about her daily routine—sometimes comforting her, sometimes making her sad.

Occasionally, when Abigail had finished her chores and was feeling adventurous, she would hike to the top of the grassy steppe, past the stone-lined well and the pear trees, past the crumbling chapel and moss-covered headstones—now so weatherworn and lichen-encrusted that the names were barely visible—and cross the perilous channel between the two land masses, clinging tightly to the ropes of the suspension bridge while trying hard not to look down.

Abigail was not fond of the bridge or the chasm. The bridge danced in the wind, shimmying and shuddering. And the razor-like rocks of Agate Gap reminded Abigail of sharks' teeth.

The view from the middle of the bridge made Abigail swoon, and she had to clutch the ropes of the railing with all her strength. Once, looking down, she saw a group of horned whales chasing prey through the Gap.

A "blessing" of Narwhal, she thought. Wondering, as the words formed in her mind, how she knew the name of the whale or that a group of Narwhal is called a "blessing." *Someone told me, I suppose.* But she couldn't exactly recall.

When the weather was calm, passage across the bridge went quickly. But when the wind was up, the way felt endless. The bridge seemed to lengthen—though Abigail was sure this was all in her mind.

The house on Indian Heath was lonelier even than Abigail's own. Dusty, too, and eerily quiet, save for the noise of the wind whistling through cracks in the walls. Even on sunny days, the rooms and hallways were dark and gloomy, and the air tasted old and stale.

The house on Indian Heath *did* have one redeeming quality. It contained books. Lots and lots of books. Apparently, the previous inhabitants had been voracious readers. Abigail was a good reader, too—

though she couldn't remember how she had learned or who had taught her. She simply knew that she liked to read.

Sometimes, she would sit by the kitchen window in the quiet little house on Indian Heath and read for hours. On other occasions, she would select a book from one of the many dusty shelves and take it carefully back across the shaky bridge, holding it tightly, not daring to look down at the rocks and waves. Once at home, she would read the book by the fire, or—if the weather was nice—on the front steps.

When she finished a book, she would always return it to Indian Heath. She didn't feel right about keeping any of the borrowed books. She read them, treated them well, and took them back, in the belief that the owner would eventually come home.

****

One day, during an unusually long rainy spell, Abigail discovered a book in the house on Indian Heath that would change everything—though she didn't realize it at the time.

The book was hidden behind other books on the uppermost corner shelf. Abigail had to stand on tiptoes on a chair, which she'd placed on top of a small table, to reach it. The book was thick and heavy in Abigail's hands, and she tottered as she hefted it, almost falling from her perch. She climbed carefully down and examined the book in the light.

The book had a dull gray cover and spine. It was nothing special. Or at least, that's what she thought at first. She blew the dust away and gasped. The cover—made of some ancient, dark wood, was set with jewels—rubies, emeralds, diamonds—and the title shimmered with gold. Real gold.

Abigail stared, wide-eyed.

"The Illustrated Guide to the Art of Dream-Weaving," she read out loud. "What on earth?"

Abigail sat on the floor, opened the book, read the first lines of the introduction, and was instantly transfixed. There she remained, lost in a trance, until it grew so dark outside that she could barely see the pages.

At last, she got to her feet, heart thumping. Her mouth was dry and her legs wobbly.

According to the book, if a person concentrated hard enough and practiced long enough, they could dream anything into existence.

Anything.

Could I dream a sister and make her real?

She opened the book again—straining to see in the dying light—and found it. The title page of the book's final chapter:

Advanced Dream-Weaving

Dreaming a Friend or Sibling to Life

There was a warning below the title, in red ink:

Caution. Virtuoso level. Proceed with care.

Abigail tucked the book inside her coat and hurried out of the house. It was raining softly, but she barely noticed. She hardly even noticed the bridge—how it bobbed and shimmied in the half-light high above the jagged rocks as she dashed across. Her mind was on the book. She was thinking, making plans.

I'll start small. Learn the basics first. Beginning dream-weaving. I'll practice and practice and practice. And then, when I've learned enough, I'll make a sister. A friend. Emily. I'll dream her to life. And I won't be lonely anymore.

****

It was dark by the time Abigail got back to her house. She set the book carefully on the kitchen table, lit a candle, and stared at the jewel-embossed cover. She wanted to open it immediately and get right to work, but she was famished. And dizzy—from all the thinking and reading she'd already done.

She made a simple dinner of broiled whitefish and peas from the garden and ate quickly, her brain spinning with a million thoughts, questions, and ideas. After the dishes were done, she lit more candles and opened the ancient book to the first chapter.

Chapter One
The Weaving of Inanimate Objects

The chapter was all about dreaming—or dream-*weaving*—simple things. Rocks. Shells. Bones. Glass.

Abigail read and contemplated. Made notes.

The house fell silent, save for the muted, rhythmic roar of the sea—a sound so familiar to Abigail that she barely noticed it—and the whispering of the candles as they fluttered and sputtered in the draft.

Hours passed. The candles burned low. And Abigail grew tired. Though she was still very excited.

I'm going to dream-weave a stone tonight, she thought, as she yawned and stretched her arms. *A skipping stone. Perfectly round. Perfectly flat. With a perfectly blue crystal right in the middle.*

From what she'd discerned of the first chapter, it sounded simple.

All she had to do was say the proper words in the proper order as she drifted off to sleep, hold the image of the stone in her mind—imagining it as clearly and precisely as possible—and then shape and mold the stone when it appeared in her dream.

Simple enough. Easy.

But it wasn't.

And it didn't work.

She slept well and deeply, all through the night. And she *did* dream of a skipping stone and of shaping and molding it in her hands. She even dreamed that she finished the stone and set it carefully in the middle of the path in front of her house—for her waking self to find in the morning.

But when, at sunrise, she threw open the front door and ran outside, there was nothing there. No stone. No artifact from the dream. Nothing.

Abigail was puzzled. Disappointed.

Why didn't it work? What did I do wrong?

She thought about it and decided that perhaps dream-weaving—even beginning dream-weaving—was harder than she'd imagined.

"I'll try it again tonight," she said resolutely. "I'll repeat the whole process."

She did.

Still, when the next morning came, nothing.

No flat skipping stone. No blue crystal.

The path in front of her door was empty.

She read the first chapter again—twice—and tried to dream-weave the stone again the next night.

And the next.

Nothing.

No stone.

Not even a *part* of a stone.

Nothing at all.

She tried again.

No luck.

Six days after discovering the book, Abigail sat on her front steps, blinking away tears.

The book is just pretend. Just a story. Make-believe. I was foolish to think such a thing could ever work.

She wept harder as she realized that Emily could never be real. *How stupid I've been.*

The tears flowed freely, and she gave up trying to hold them back.

No sister.

No Emily.

Not even a silly skipping stone.

Abigail—blessed as she was with the ability to find the good and the positive in almost any situation—rarely got discouraged. But she was discouraged now.

She cried for a long time, until she couldn't cry anymore. Then she got to her feet and decided abruptly, angrily that she was sick of the stupid book and wanted it out of her house. Immediately.

She glanced outside. Afternoon light streamed golden through her windows, and the sun—a blinding molten ball on the horizon—appeared to be sinking into the sea.

I'll return it in the morning.

She had no desire to cross the creaking, swaying bridge in the dark.

****

Night came.

And as she made dinner, for the first time in a week, Abigail thought about things other than dream-weaving.

She thought about her garden, and her favorite

walks, and her animal friends—whom, she realized, she'd been neglecting. *I'll visit them tomorrow*, she told herself.

The idea of tending her garden and seeing her animal friends made her feel better.

She got ready for bed, still not thinking about the book. She brushed her teeth, filled a glass of water for her bedside table, fluffed her pillows, and climbed under the covers.

As she was drifting peacefully off to sleep, Abigail decided—randomly and spontaneously—to give dream-weaving one last try.

She smiled to her half-conscious self, almost laughing at the silliness of it.

It won't work.

It's ridiculous.

It's pretend.

Abigail's breathing slowed. Her eyelids fluttered. She mumbled the words she'd memorized and pictured the skipping stone—a lovely flat one with a blue crystal—holding the image in her mind.

Of course, it will never work.

Never work.

Never ...

She laughed. Rolled over. And fell into a deeper sleep.

****

Abigail awoke, refreshed, with no memory whatsoever of her dreams.

She dressed and stretched and shoved back the curtains, revealing a vast silvery sea and an endless blue sky.

It's going to be a nice day.

She dressed, turned on the teakettle, and opened the front door to let in the fresh sea air.

And froze.

There, in the middle of the path, lay the stone.

The skipping stone.

Bright and new in the morning sun. Like a gift.

The skipping stone with the blue crystal in the center.

Abigail stood very still, afraid to move.

It's real. A dream creation come to life.

She knelt, hands trembling, and picked up the stone. Stared at it. Felt its weight. Lifted it to the light. Marveled at its smoothness and flatness, at the sparkle of the crystal embedded precisely in the middle.

It's exactly as I imagined. It's just what I pictured.

She held the stone in her outstretched hand, expecting it to dissolve. Evaporate. Disappear. Back into the world of dreams.

But it did not dissolve. The stone was real.

As real as the steppe.

As real as the house.

As real as the cliffs. The sea. The sun.

As real as me, Abigail thought, still in shock.

Not pretend.

Dream-weaving actually works.

It works!

Then …

If I can make a stone … I can make other things.

A bush. A tree. A bird.

A sister.

Emily.

****

From that moment on, Abigail worked extra hard.

She studied patiently. Intently. Tenaciously.

She pored over the pages of *The Illustrated Guide to the Art of Dream-Weaving* day after day, memorizing the poems and chants and songs, whispering the words as she went about her routine.

At night, Abigail dreamed. And her talent blossomed and burned like the full moon over a black sea.

She made a bird—bright gold, with emerald top feathers. It could say a single word: *Abigail.*

She made a clam. A sunfish. A seal. A red fox.

She thought at first that the things she made might fade after a few days, but they did not. They seemed, if anything, to become more real with time.

The clam dug a hole and vanished into the beach sand, just like an ordinary clam. The bird built a nest on one of the cliffs, and sometimes Abigail caught sight of it flying over her house at sunset. The fox joined other foxes on the steppe—running and playing, hunting, and sunning itself in the tall grass.

The seal—a lovely gray harbor seal with long whiskers and a sweet, endearing face—swam close to Abigail when she sat on the rocks of the breakwater. It stared at her curiously, as if trying to recall where it had seen her before. Then it swam away to join a large group of other pinnipeds hunting for salmon.

The encounter left Abigail feeling happy—and sad. Happy to see her creation flourishing. Sad to see it leave.

****

After months of careful, thoughtful practice, Abigail believed she was ready to begin dream-weaving a sister. Emily.

She'd learned through trial and error that the more complex dream creations took many nights and many dreams, one after another, to complete.

The bird had taken her six nights. The fox, two weeks. The seal, a month.

It will take a year to dream Emily properly. Maybe longer.

No matter. She vowed to spend whatever time was necessary. She would be patient. She would get everything exactly right. There would be no shortcuts.

She made notes as she read the chapters on advanced dream-weaving again. She pondered and contemplated.

This is it, she thought at last, on a day when the sky was dark and brooding and the sea blue-green and churning. *Tonight, I can begin.*

****

When she finally went to bed that evening, she slept deeply, and her sleeping brain thrummed and hummed.

She dreamed first that she was standing in a darkened meadow. The air smelled of grass and flowers gone to sleep. The silent, fathomless sky blazed with the white fire of innumerable stars.

Abigail stared into the blackness, seeing nothing, wondering why she was there.

"Who am I?" asked a faint, frightened voice somewhere in the void. Abigail jumped.

"You are Emily," Abigail replied after a long moment. Though she could not see the speaker, she knew who was talking as surely as she knew her own reflection. "You are my sister."

"Emily," the voice said carefully, as if it were a

newly invented word.

"Yes."

The invisible speaker fell silent and did not talk again that night.

****

The dream encounter played in Abigail's mind throughout the following day, and the second night's dream unfolded in the same dark field as the first.

Abigail's dream-self stood in the grass as before, alert and aware, gazing at the sky, seeking familiar constellations.

Abigail knew the planets and stars and loved looking at the heavens, especially on warm summer nights when the sea was calm and the breeze gentle. It unsettled her greatly that, in this dream, she could discern not a single recognizable constellation. These skies were strange. Incomprehensible.

There was something else disturbing about the dream. An absence, stark and terrifying. It hit Abigail suddenly, like a slap across the face.

The sound of the sea—Abigail's faithful, constant, lifelong companion—was missing. She shivered. *Where's the ocean. Where am I?*

The grass around Abigail rustled in the darkness, and Emily's voice startled her again, asking, "Why am I awake?"

Abigail took a deep breath. The question struck her as funny, considering that she herself was asleep and dreaming, but she did not laugh. "I thought of you," she said gently, "because I was lonely. And now we're talking. I hope you don't mind being awake."

"No," said the voice. "I don't mind."

The voice fell silent and did not speak again, but

the question stuck in Abigail's head. *Why am I awake?*

Is that what's happening here? Is this what dream-weaving really is? The waking of things that already exist? The nudging and cajoling of spirits asleep?

It was a riddle she could not solve.

****

The dreams continued this way for weeks, each encounter slightly longer than the last, each conversation building on topics that she and Emily had discussed before. Steady progress, night after night.

Still, there was only a disembodied voice in the darkness—no *person* that Abigail could see. Nevertheless, the encounters were becoming more vivid, more substantial, as if, with each interaction, Emily was becoming more real. More *awake*.

During each dream, Emily asked questions, and Abigail told her what she could about the world. About Agate Gap and Indian Heath and the terrifying violence of the Breaking. About the animals and plants and the surging sea.

Abigail's dream-self wanted to approach the voice and embrace the speaker, but something held her back. Something deep inside told her it wasn't yet time. That making contact prematurely could ruin everything.

****

After weeks of patient, careful dream-weaving, it occurred to Abigail one morning that she had not visited the house on Indian Heath for a long time. The realization alarmed her—she considered herself the home's caretaker after all—and she resolved to go and check on things that very afternoon.

Afternoon came, and Abigail climbed the hill behind her house and approached the spindly bridge, which was trembling and shimmying above the chasm like a twig in the breeze.

The lonely house was there, on the far side of the bridge. Same as ever.

Same as ever, Abigail told herself.

Except not quite.

Abigail stared at the forlorn house, suddenly afraid.

"She's there," Abigail gasped, knowing it was true. *Emily is inside that house. Sleeping.*

Becoming.

Abigail had no idea *how* she knew that this was true but knew it in the very marrow of her bones all the same.

Emily is there.

Forming. Growing. Taking shape. Deep in sleep and not yet ready to wake.

Abigail perceived also that to look upon her sister in this early, nascent stage would be to risk everything.

She waited, paralyzed, trembling like the bridge itself, breathing in and out. She had an almost overwhelming desire to sprint across the chasm and enter the house. But a countervailing impulse kept her glued to the ground.

I can only see her in my dreams right now. Only in my dreams—until she wakes, when the time is right.

A fragment of a memory, vague and troubling, surfaced in Abigail's mind.

Waking her now might cause ...

Might cause ...

"No," Abigail said out loud, terminating the black thoughts. She turned and walked home.

Emily's there—inside the house on Indian Heath. And the time is not yet right.

****

Patiently, steadily, faithfully, Abigail kept dreaming. And dream-weaving.

Months passed. Seasons. And Abigail's loneliness grew.

I need to have faith, Abigail told herself. *I need to be steadfast.*

And she was.

And then one morning, very abruptly, Abigail sensed that things had changed. That the time had come.

This is it, she thought, as she sat up in bed and swung her feet to the floor. *This is the day. Emily is ready to rise.*

****

Bursting with anticipation and struggling to contain it in case she was wrong, Abigail went about her morning routine. Then she climbed the hill behind her house and approached the spindly bridge—presently hanging motionless in the calm morning air—and sat down on a rock on her side of the chasm. An ideal spot to view the lonely house on Indian Heath without getting too close.

She waited and watched.

The sun climbed higher.

Swallows darted through the bright sky, under and over and around the bridge. An incoming tide flooded the gorge, covering the knife-edged rocks. Sea lions bellowed, and waves pummeled the outer coast, rumbling rhythmically, like the heart of an immense living thing.

Abigail waited.

Maybe I was wrong. Maybe this isn't the day.

Maybe Emily's not even there.

And then the light changed minutely, and the front door of the Indian Heath house swung inward. A girl stepped out, onto the porch, then into the tall grass. She stood in the sun, face uplifted.

Abigail's heart leapt, and she got to her feet. "Emily!" she cried.

The girl squinted and smiled. "Abigail?"

She knows my name.

They ran toward each other and met in the middle of the bridge—Abigail so overcome with emotion that she forgot her fear of the chasm.

The girls embraced and held hands. Laughed and looked at each other and embraced again.

"Sister," said Abigail, unable to contain her joy, "it's good to see you."

"It's good to be awake," said Emily with a slightly puzzled look. "I … I hope I haven't kept you waiting, Abigail."

Abigail dismissed the comment with a laugh and a wave. "You're here now. That's all that matters. Come. Let me show you around."

Thus, began the happiest chapter of Abigail's life.

****

The girls became immediate best friends. Emily moved into Abigail's house, and they did everything together. Played and sang and talked. Worked and read and laughed—especially laughed. Emily and Abigail laughed *a lot.*

Which is not to say that everything was always wonderful or that Abigail and Emily never disagreed. In fact, they disagreed often. As Abigail soon learned, Emily had a will of her own, with strong opinions, likes, and dislikes.

Abigail was a morning person who preferred to go to bed early. Emily, a night owl, liked staying up late—sometimes very late—to read or to look at the stars. Abigail enjoyed bright, sunny days. Emily loved rain and storms. Abigail was afraid of the dark and the shimmying bridge to Indian Heath. Emily was fearless when it came to these things but wary of the ocean and unnerved by worms and spiders.

Abigail found the differences between herself and her sibling immensely encouraging. Clearly, Emily was a unique individual with her own mind and identity—not merely a reflection of her weaver.

****

It dawned on Abigail after they met that Emily didn't know about her true nature or origin. She had expected her sister to ask questions. *How did I get here? Why was I in the house on Indian Heath? Where was I before this?* But she didn't.

Instead, it seemed to Abigail that her sister believed she had always been there.

And indeed, from the first moments, it was clear that Emily knew much about her surroundings. She knew the meandering trails and the layout and quirks of each house. She knew what was growing in the garden and the names of the birds and animals. She knew about the tides and the weather and the phases of the moon.

This familiarity with the world struck Abigail as odd at first, but it made sense when she considered it.

Born of my dreams, she has my knowledge—or much of it. I didn't dream a baby after all. I dreamed someone roughly my age, and we conversed inside the dreams, at length. So, of course she can talk and think and find her way around.

Still, Abigail found Emily's apparent obliviousness to her past—and her lack of curiosity—a little unsettling. She wondered if she should tell her sister that she'd dreamed her to life. She pondered the question long and hard. And decided against it.

She seems happy. And I certainly am. Why risk upsetting her? Why risk ruining things just as our relationship is starting? I can always tell her later. Someday. If I need to.

Nevertheless, doubt lingered in Abigail's mind, and she referred to *The Illustrated Guide to the Art of Dream-Weaving*, which she'd been keeping under her bed, for advice. She found nothing concerning how to tell someone they were dreamed into existence—or whether it was even necessary to do so—but she did discover a curious notation on the final page. A bit of text she'd somehow missed in all her earlier readings.

A dream creation, properly woven, will be indistinguishable from others of its kind, save for one characteristic. Dream creations cannot be harmed by lightning.

Abigail read the passage again, and her worries subsided. *Cannot be harmed by lightning? So ... the only way Emily can discover her true nature—unless, of course, I tell her—is if she gets struck by lightning and doesn't die?*

Abigail laughed at the silliness of it. The odds of being hit by lightning were absurdly remote. *Ridiculous,* she told herself.

She thought about returning the book to the house on Indian Heath, where it belonged, then decided to wait. Having the book nearby seemed like a good idea, and she slid it back under her bed. *There's no rush. I have plenty of time.*

She was wrong. Time was running out very quickly indeed.

****

The days grew shorter and the weather cooler with the coming of autumn. Rain poured from the sky in an endless, drumming drizzle, turning familiar trails into muddy streamlets. Peering out at the granite-gray horizon, it was impossible to know where the sky ended and the sea began.

Far from feeling sad about the weather, though, Abigail was as happy as she'd ever been. With Emily to talk to and play with, the dreary rains of autumn and the raging storms of winter became an adventure. On long nights, during the approach of the solstice, they played games by the fire or read passages from favorite books. They talked of what they would grow in the garden come spring and told stories about the myriad creatures that shared their home. In the mornings—even on cold, blustery days—they fished and dug clams and roamed the beaches in search of treasure and messages from the wider world.

Winter passed, the land awoke from its sleep, and Abigail's contentment swelled.

Trees greened. Flowers bloomed. Baby river otters tumbled from cozy dens above the beach. And birds— yellow warblers, violet-green swallows, bluebirds, spotted towhees, and more—returned from far away, filling the air with song.

Abigail and Emily readied the gardens and repaired the washed-out paths. They cleaned the house from top to bottom—even the roof and fireplace. And on a bright, sunny May morning, they trekked together to the other house, on Indian Heath, and flung open the windows and doors, releasing the stale, stagnant air.

Crossing the chasm back to their own meadow, they ran laughing through the tall grass, dancing and twirling and chasing butterflies in the warm spring sunshine.

The girls paused below the crest of the ridge overlooking the eastern shore to observe a family of foxes. It was a group they knew and loved and encountered regularly.

Standing alongside her sister, Abigail watched the foxes, and her ebullience dimmed. The foxes were working—frantically, furiously—on strengthening and fortifying their den. Not a typical activity for a bright spring day.

Abigail took her sister's hand, and together they walked to the top of the ridge. There they stood staring, awestruck.

The sun was still shining, but the sky to the east had become a wall of billowing clouds—blue-black and darkening as they watched, like a terrible bruise spreading fast. The sea below the clouds—pale green, shot with bolts of deep violet—seemed oddly, disquietingly serene.

The hush before the fury, Abigail thought, recalling something from earliest childhood.

The girls stood their ground, saying nothing. More clouds drifted in to join the metastasizing mass, like patrols returning to the main host.

"We need to get ready," Abigail whispered. "Prepare the house."

Emily looked at her sister. "You scared, Abi?"

Abigail shrugged. "A little." She tried to sound calm and in control. "I've never seen a sky quite like this one. I mean, not since I was little."

****

The storm came swiftly, blotting out the sun and raking the steppe with increasingly fierce gusts of wind. Enormous waves smashed the coastline, and the temperature dropped twenty degrees.

Abigail and Emily hurried back to their house and secured as much as they could. They covered the fragile new garden plants and closed and latched the shutters. They brought in chairs and tables and reattached a gutter that had come loose.

Rain spattered the roof tiles as they worked—big heavy drops, at first, that hissed like grease in a frying pan.

By the time they finished, the rain had become a drenching downpour, and the girls' hair and clothing were soaked.

"We'll build a fire," said Abigail as they pushed through the front door and stood dripping on the smooth stone entry. "Dry out these wet …" She stopped.

"What is it?" Emily asked. "Abi, what's wrong?"

"The house on Indian Heath. We left everything open. All the windows and doors."

Emily nodded but said nothing. She looked frightened.

"It will flood," said Abigail. "The books will be ruined. How stupid of me."

"It's my fault, too," said Emily. "I helped open it up."

Abigail smiled, buoyed by her sister's words. "I'll

go," she said. "Over and back. There's still time."

"I'll come with you."

"No," said Abigail. "You mustn't. This house needs watching, too, and you're in charge while I'm away."

"But …"

"Get a fire going. I'll be right back."

Abigail hugged her sister and ducked out the door and into the raging storm.

****

Abigail struggled up the hill to the bridge, marveling at how the world had changed since morning.

The wind was now so strong that she could barely stand. Rain cascaded down, hurled this way and that in great whipping waves, as if the sea itself had moved inland. Peering out from under her hood, Abigail found it impossible to see more than a few feet ahead. But she knew the way and plodded on, determined to protect the house on Indian Heath.

Water ran in myriad rivulets, gurgling beneath Abigail's feet. The wind screamed and the ocean boomed. She hoped all of her animal friends were okay.

She climbed on, bent almost double against the wind. The trail leveled out, and she followed it to the chasm, where the cacophony increased. The wind was driving enormous amounts of seawater through the narrow gorge, pounding the rocks and sending great geysers of salty spray high into the air. Abigail raised her eyes and stopped, terrified.

The bridge stretched before her, whipping and bucking like a snake tossed into a fire. The Indian Heath house was a dim box on the far side. Barely discernible. She watched the bridge, wondering if the structure's undulations might subside between gusts, wondering if she could time it right, wondering if it was even possible to make the passage.

She thought about turning for home. Giving up. She heard a *bang* and realized it was coming from the far house. The front door—which they'd left standing open not two hours earlier—was flapping in the wind. The shutters, too. *Bang, bang, bang.*

The house will be destroyed, Abigail thought. And without further reflection, she made a dash for it, sprinting with all her strength and will.

****

Near the middle of the bridge, Abigail experienced a terrifying revelation. Indian Heath—the entire steppe—was moving away, pulling on the bridge, stretching it to the breaking point. Even over the rain and screaming wind, she could hear the separation, like immense bones cracking.

The stretching was making the bridge flatter and easier to cross. *But what if it snaps? What if this is another Breaking, like long ago?*

Feet sliding on the rain-drenched slats of the bridge, she stopped running and was about to turn around when a stupendously bright flash lit the sky. Thunder boomed directly overhead.

Lightning on my heels. No choice but to keep going.

She dove into the wet grass on Indian Heath just as the bridge disintegrated and the structure whipped away and down, into the geysers of spray.

"No!" cried Abigail, as the sky exploded again, the lightning so close this time that she could smell it.

Thunder rumbled and the ground shook.

She staggered on, toward the lonely house.

Boom! Lightning blasted a tree a few paces to her right, and the uppermost branches burst into flame. Sparks hissed, and shards of burning wood whickered through the air.

Crack!

Another stupendous bolt. Searing, blinding. Nothing but whiteness all around.

She stumbled on. Two more steps. Three. The door of the Indian Heath house stood open, and the interior of the place—from what she could see—looked okay. Not destroyed. Not yet.

Another step, and lightning struck Abigail full force. Full strength. A staggeringly powerful bolt that cut the sky and charred the earth as it passed through her body.

She kept moving, utterly unscathed, onto the steps of the porch.

I'm alive, she thought absently.

The lightning hadn't harmed her.

Trail to the Sky

Wanderings

The argument broke out three miles into the hike and got ugly fast.

My brother Trevor and I were a couple hundred yards behind the women, talking about everything. Our parents. Life since college. Work. Girlfriends.

Trevor said something irritating about Heidi and Katherine—the women I'd invited on the hike. Then he insulted me. I insulted him back and said a couple of things I shouldn't have. Pushed the knife in a little deeper, as family so easily can. Told him he was crazy.

We stopped walking, and the insults got nastier. Pretty soon we were shouting. Shoving.

I caught a glimpse of Heidi and Katherine pausing, peering back through the trees—no doubt trying to figure out what all the commotion was about.

The scuffle intensified, and then Trevor and I dropped our heavy backpacks on the ground and squared off, ready to kill each other.

"Aw, screw this shit," said Trevor, lowering his fists. "I'm not putting up with your bullshit for the next three days."

"Dude," I said, "*my* bullshit?"

My brother yanked stuff out of his pack and tossed it onto the trail—stove, fuel canisters, freeze-dried dinners.

"What the hell's wrong with you?" I asked.

"Fuck off."

He shouldered his pack and glared at me a

moment, like he was debating something. Maybe another insult.

Then he shook his head and marched off, the way we'd just come. "Have a great hike, little brother."

He never looked back.

It was the second-to-the-last time I would see my brother alive and the last time we would ever talk.

Thinking back, I wish to God I'd gone with him then—that we'd walked together straight to the car, driven home, and burned the little book. But I had no inkling of the events to come.

****

Heidi and Katherine joined me moments after the argument ended, and together we watched Trevor fade into the rain-forest gloom. Heidi asked where he was going.

I shook my head. "Home, apparently."

"What happened, Jake?" Katherine inquired gently.

"Nothing. Just a stupid argument. About nothing. Brothers, you know?" I stared after Trevor, half expecting to see him making his way back to apologize. But there was no sign of him. No sign of anyone.

The forest grew quiet once more, save for the sound of trickling water. Little brown birds flitted among the ferns and salal.

Katherine sighed. "Should we head back, too, then? Bag it?"

"Heck, no," I replied. "He's got his own car. No reason that idiot should ruin the trip for the rest of us."

I regarded the women. We'd only just met in person a week earlier, after a few exchanges on Facebook, and our debut outing together was not going at all as I had planned. "Unless you guys want to turn back," I said.

Heidi and Katherine looked at each other. Shrugged. "I want to keep going," said Heidi.

"Me, too," said Katherine. "I've really been looking forward to this."

I smiled. "Cool. Let's do it, then."

Trevor's insane. Heidi and Katherine were beautiful. Smart. Athletic. They both seemed really nice. My mind drifted into a blissful fantasy—and not for the first time that morning. The fantasy involved what might happen after we got to our destination, a remote mountain lake. *We'll set up camp. Go for a swim. Eat dinner and drink some wine. Watch the sunset. Then Heidi and Katherine will invite me into their tent, and ...*

"Jake," said Heidi, ending my reverie. "Did you keep the little guidebook, or did Trevor take it with him?" She smiled as she asked the question, her tone casual and light, but there was an odd intensity in her gaze.

I patted a side pouch on my pack. "I have it. Double-ziplocked and bubble-wrapped."

"Oh, that's great," she said. "It'll be fun to check out those maps later."

I thought so, too.

****

I surveyed the items Trevor had dumped on the trail. We'd divided the supplies the night before, at Trevor's apartment in Seattle. I'd agreed to carry the satellite phone and the tent. He'd taken the stove, three fuel canisters, and much of the food—packed tightly in a bear-resistant container. Now, I had to somehow get his crap into my already full—and heavy—pack. It seemed impossible—until I gave my lithe, long-legged hiking partners another look and realized I'd figure it out. If the pack weighed two hundred pounds, I'd figure it out.

****

A few minutes later, we were moving again along the Deception Ridge Trail, deeper into the cool rain forest.

As I explained to my companions, most parties following the trail head for Red Meadows or High Bridge Basin, on the flanks of Phantom Spire about ten miles in. It was a path I'd traveled many times with family and friends.

Our plan for this trip was different. We'd follow the main trail for five miles, then peel off at Graves Crossing and bushwhack along the eastern bank of Deception Creek to the start of a little-used and far more difficult trail known as—in the few guidebooks that even bothered to include it—the Torch Lake Trace. I'd been on the trace once, years earlier, with Trevor and our dad, and I remembered it being a brutally steep, nearly technical ascent. A quadriceps-torturing grind, terminating—after an interminable climb—in a pristine alpine basin graced with lush flower-filled meadows and a perfect cobalt-blue glacial cirque.

The guidebooks had warned that the trace was unmaintained, difficult to follow, and subject to damage from slides and washouts. "Advanced route-finding and mountaineering skills recommended," admonished one book. Even simply locating the trace was no easy matter. I remembered my dad and brother and I stomping around in the underbrush for an hour, looking for the start of the path.

I'd told Heidi and Katherine all about the difficulties of the Torch Lake Trace—the brutal climb, the sketchy trail conditions. I didn't want them to be surprised—or pissed off. But both seemed excited about the challenge and up for the adventure. And on Facebook, both had said they'd done plenty of backpacking and climbing and enjoyed wilderness travel.

My kind of women.

****

We stopped for a snack at Graves Crossing—near the new suspension bridge over Deception Creek—and sat together on a log beneath enormous old-growth fir and cedar trees. There was no one else around. In fact, we'd seen only one other party since the start of the trip. Unusual, I thought, for a sunny July weekend.

We talked and shared our food—salami, cheese, dark chocolate, trail mix. The creek rumbled and roared at our feet, flowing fast and full with snowmelt. Mist wafted from the churning water.

I unfolded a Green Trails map, and Heidi and Katherine crowded in on either side of me to have a look.

Katherine undid her ponytail—presumably so she could retie it—and shook her head, liberating magnificent handfuls of thick, dark hair.

Her hair smelled like flowers, and the fragrance—combined with the citrusy scent of her skin, warm from the hike—almost made me forget what day it was.

The map, the map, I said to myself.

My brain reengaged, and I showed them our current location, how far we'd come, where we'd find the start of the Torch Lake Trace. The trace itself I had drawn in blue pen.

Torch Lake was on the map—a tiny blue dot amid violently zigzagging lines denoting peaks and ridges, fissures and plateaus. But as far as Green Trails was concerned, the trace didn't exist.

Heidi leaned close, studying the route intently. She and Katherine had both seen the map before—a week earlier, at a Starbucks in Ballard—when we'd all met in person for the first time.

"What about the 'mystery trail'?" she asked brightly. "And that *other* map of yours?"

"Let's take a look," I replied.

I opened the side pouch of my pack, withdrew the double-bagged heirloom within, and slowly, carefully, unwrapped it.

I could've shown them the photocopied pages instead. Limited it to that. I wish now that I had. But the actual journal was undeniably cooler. More impressive. And I wanted very much to impress my new friends.

****

The journal was old. Small. Bound in creased, cracked leather the color of Martian soil. It smelled like a museum. A long-undisturbed attic.

It had a leather tie on the right-hand side and a tiny, embossed mountain on the front but was otherwise unadorned. I didn't recognize the mountain—it wasn't the Matterhorn or Everest or Rainier. Nothing iconic. Still, it caught the eye. There was something ominous about it. Something unsettling.

I'd examined the journal before, of course—but it looked different in the open air. More substantial somehow.

Must be the light.

The journal *felt* different in my hands, too. Heavier. Thicker. As if lead weights had been sewn into the binding.

I ignored these things.

Paid no attention.

Opened the book.

****

The world changed then—I understand that now. Everything shifted, ever so slightly.

The fabric of the cosmos quivered. Gently. Like a spiderweb nicked by a raindrop.

I didn't notice.

Had I been listening, paying attention, I might have heard a deviation in the sound of the water rolling over the stones at my feet. Or sensed the quiet gnashing of tectonic plates hundreds of miles underground. Perceived the muting of the light all around us or the sighing of the trees.

I know now that the unraveling began as soon as I opened the book. No way to stop it or turn back the clock.

****

Together Heidi, Katherine, and I stared at the words penciled on the first page—a single bold thought followed by some mundane details in a smaller script:

Going to the mountains is going home.

Property of John Muir

Martinez, California

If found, please return.

"What a treasure," said Katherine.

I nodded. "I know." We lingered over the words and the handwriting, and then I turned carefully to a bookmark halfway through the little journal.

Gracing this section—hand-drawn maps adorned with beautiful, intricate renderings of peaks and valleys, glaciers and waterfalls, meadows and trails.

"This must be a really old trail." Heidi lifted her eyes from the journal to the path we'd just walked.

"It is. My dad did quite a bit of research after he found the journal in my grandfather's things. Deception Ridge Trail was made by indigenous people, apparently. Native Americans. Probably here for hundreds of years before John Muir ever set foot on it."

I laid the little journal on top of the official map, and we compared the routes.

Muir's beautiful pencil sketches—showing Deception Creek, the trail, and nearby peaks and passes—clearly matched the other map.

"This is where we are now," I said, pointing to Graves Crossing on both maps. "And this is where we're headed." I followed Muir's sketched trail with my fingertip an inch or so farther, to the start of the Torch Lake Trace—a dotted line terminating in a high alpine meadow. A simple, artful depiction of a mountain lake lay in the center of the meadow.

"According to my dad," I said, "it wasn't named Torch Lake until the 1920s. But clearly Muir knew about it."

"Did Muir build the trace?" asked Katherine.

I shook my head. "It was probably just a game trail. Or maybe Native Americans visited the lake to hunt and fish."

In the margin, there was a handwritten notation:

Reached mid-mountain in a tempestuous wind attended by spectacular thunder and lightning, the temperature at once mild and invigorating.

"And here," I said, with mock gravity, "is the mystery trail." I pointed to a spot in the middle of Muir's map, where a side trail split from the trace itself. "The holy grail of our trip."

The line representing the mystery trail veered sharply away from the trace, exited Muir's elegant drawing, crossed the gutter of the little journal, and vanished amid a blur of erasures and smudges on the facing page.

"What was on this page?" Katherine asked.

"No clue," I replied. "Apparently, Muir was unhappy with his artwork and got rid of it."

"Or," said Heidi conspiratorially, "he didn't want anyone to see what he'd found at the end of that trail."

I nodded. Laughed. "Exactly."

"You saw *this*, right?" Katherine pointed at a drawing of a boulder at the spot where the mystery trail split from the trace. "When you were with your dad and brother?"

"Definitely. Can't miss the rock. Thing's as big as a school bus. What we didn't see was any kind of spur trail."

"But," said Katherine hopefully, "you didn't have the journal last time you hiked up there, right?"

"No. Didn't even *know* about the journal. My dad didn't find it 'til last year, after my grandfather passed away."

"So you weren't exactly looking for a spur trail," said Heidi. "Maybe it *is* there but just hidden."

"Possible," I said. "I *hope* it's there. Though, as I told you guys last week, there's nothing about a trail in that location in any book or on any maps that I've seen—or even on Google Earth."

"Strath ay Banrigh," Katherine said haltingly, struggling to pronounce a notation scrawled beneath the mystery trail.

"Gaelic," I said. "For 'Valley of the Queen.' We looked it up."

"Strath ay Banrigh," Heidi repeated.

"Muir was a Scot," I said, as if that explained everything.

Katherine peered upstream—the direction we were about to walk. "*Is* there a place out here called Strath ay Banrigh, or whatever—Valley of the Queen?"

I laughed. "No, unfortunately. Nothing even close. We checked that, as well."

There was one more notation on the map—this one at the bottom of the page, small and compact and in plain English.

13 May 1902—Shared discovery with TR at Surniff Glen this morning. Disbelieved my account at first. Questioned my mental fitness and asked if I had been drinking. Cannot fault him. Came around once I showed him evidence, then cancelled his other meetings and wanted to know all. Promised quick action. Holloway present throughout—though I had requested a private audience. This I regret deeply. Cannot stand the fellow and do not trust him.

"'TR' is the president," Katherine said matter-of-factly.

I nodded. "Teddy Roosevelt. He and Muir were friends and worked together on conservation projects and some of the first national parks. Holloway was Luther Holloway, a rep for the timber industry. Apparently, Muir wasn't too happy he was in the meeting."

****

The women seemed genuinely interested in the research my dad and Trevor and I had done. They speculated about what Muir might have said to Roosevelt—and why Muir had fretted about Luther Holloway's presence at the meeting all those years ago. And they asked me a ton of questions, though as I discovered later, they already knew many of the answers—knew far more about the whole situation than I did, in fact.

They were acting. Drawing me in. Bringing me along. They needed me—at least for a few more hours.

****

I put the book away, and we started bushwhacking along the creek to the junction with the Torch Lake Trace. Our plan was to locate the trace and climb toward the lake—stopping at the boulder halfway up to search for evidence of Muir's mystery trail. I was looking forward to the search. It was an adventure. A treasure hunt. But I seriously doubted we'd find anything.

The good news—as far as I was concerned—was that it didn't really matter. After exploring around the boulder, we'd climb on up to Torch Lake—one of the most sublime places in all of the Olympic Mountains—and set up camp. I thought for sure my companions would be impressed with the views and scenery. I thought we'd arrive with the sun still high in the sky, with plenty of time to swim and bask on the rocks before turning in for the night.

It didn't work out that way.

****

As we departed Graves Crossing, I looked back the

way we'd come—hoping to see Trevor on the trail, hurrying to catch up with us. I imagined greeting him with some brotherly profanity and joking about the asinine argument earlier. I imagined us shaking hands and putting the whole stupid incident behind us, carrying on with our trip, and having a great time.

Stare as I might, though, there was no sign of my brother. Just empty, lonely trail and silent, still forest.

****

We made our way along the creek edge, through a waist-high sea of ferns and salal, huckleberry and rhododendron. We were far up-valley now—not in the heart of the Olympic Mountains yet, but close. Verdant forested slopes rose thousands of feet on either side of us, and the air tasted clean and fresh.

I knew from the trip I'd taken with Trevor and our dad that the trace originated in a small clearing about a mile from Graves Crossing. Sure enough, the clearing was right where I remembered it—unchanged, as far as I could tell. The trace was there, too—just a faint indentation in the grass—the ghost of a real trail. It would've been easy to miss.

We stood in the little clearing, and I followed the "ghost trail" with my eyes. It led away into the trees and straight uphill.

A bit higher, the forest was interspersed with steep scree fields—broad swaths of boulders and debris fanning down from snow-covered Mount Sperling— and, here and there, fragments of the trace were visible against the mountainside, like tiny pale scars.

"Now for the fun part," I said, tightening the straps on my pack and readying my hiking poles. A few clouds hovered over the valley, but the sun cut through, filling our little creek-side meadow with golden summer light. It was early still and cool. Perfect hiking weather.

"Let's do it," said Heidi, and together the three of us plunged into the forest and up the first steep incline.

Within minutes, my heart was thumping. My thighs burning.

Most trails ascend sharp inclines via switchbacks, but the builders of the Torch Lake Trace had clearly opted for a more direct approach—namely, going straight uphill.

Hoisting ourselves up the thirty-five-degree slope—over and around roots and rocks and fallen trees—conversation ceased. We focused on our breathing, on the next handhold or boot placement, on moving higher, step by step. We fell into a rhythm.

After thirty minutes of hard slogging, we entered another break in the trees, paused on a small level patch of ground, and discovered that we were already high above Deception Creek.

The valley—lush, unroaded, and unspoiled—lay below like a panorama in a nineteenth-century watercolor.

I breathed in and out, savoring the moment. It was good to be back in the wilderness—on temporary hiatus from the "civilized" world.

My parents started taking me and Trevor backpacking when we were toddlers, so I feel connected to wild places. Happy and content when I'm miles from the nearest road.

Trevor.

I wished he was there to share the view. I pictured him driving home. Pissed off. Regretting the way the morning had ended.

****

We rested in the tiny clearing—Heidi, Katherine, and I—admiring the valley, the river, the jagged, precipitous slope across the way. Hawks pirouetted overhead. Waterfalls sparkled and flashed in the sun like tinsel.

Then the view changed.

The flashing diminished. Our side of the valley fell into shadow, and a chill breeze wafted down from on high.

"Whoa," said Katherine, gazing skyward. "Looks like we might need the rain gear after all."

****

A fat gray cloud now lay against the mountainside above us, blocking the sun.

Craning our necks, we could see where the trace vanished into the fog.

"Probably burn off by the time we get up there," I said hopefully as the light on our side of the valley continued to dim.

We hadn't noticed the cloud until now, but that didn't mean anything. We'd been in the trees most of the day, and weather in the Olympics is notoriously fickle. Sunny, warm mornings often mutate into cold, wet—even snowy—afternoons, and every area guidebook warns hikers to dress in layers, bring extra clothes, and prepare for rain.

"Even if it doesn't burn off," Katherine said, "I bet we hike right through it."

"I like your attitude," I replied.

****

Slogging uphill, gasping for breath, I noticed with

some irritation that the opposite side of the valley was still sunny. Cloud-free.

The hovering cloud above us did not burn off. If anything, it grew in density and mass the nearer we got. From a hundred feet away, it resembled an upside-down ocean, cool and gray, daring us to approach.

We trudged on until we were directly beneath the cloud—until we could literally reach up and touch it. Feel the moisture on our hands and faces. According to my watch, we'd climbed 1,400 feet since the river.

"It's amazing," said Heidi, eyes sparkling as she surveyed the flat gray ceiling.

I nodded. "It really is. Such an abrupt transition. I've hiked in fog plenty of times, but this is …"

"Freaky?" said Katherine.

"I was going to say 'cool,' but 'freaky' is accurate."

Ten feet farther on, the trace vanished into the cloud, like a ladder to another world.

My skin tingled. My heart pattered and thrummed. I would have opted for sunshine, of course, but the cloud—such an unusual cloud—represented fun. Something unexpected.

Katherine regarded our path doubtfully. "We're gonna want to stay on the trail," she whispered.

I nodded. "We'll be fine. I'll bet we're through this thing in twenty minutes."

****

As we climbed into the mist, the temperature fell ten degrees. Shimmering, iridescent dewdrops coalesced on our hair, clothing, packs.

Heidi took the lead, Katherine followed, and I came last, struggling under the extra weight of my pack.

Visibility dropped to twenty feet, then ten, as silent gray tentacles of fog flowed around us. Enveloped us.

The trace grew slippery, but we stepped carefully, and the path was surprisingly easy to follow. It materialized, one short segment at a time, before our eyes, then vanished into the mist after we had passed. Rocks, trees, and wildflowers appeared as we ascended, glowing like phosphorescent highway markers, then fading into the gloom.

My hearing grew more acute as visibility diminished. I could hear the soil sloughing beneath my boots; the rhythmic, labored breathing of my companions; water trickling over stone somewhere nearby.

The sounds were soothing, reassuring.

Then there was another sound from high above—a deep and distant rumble, like far-off thunder.

We froze, and the rumble intensified, morphing into a symphony of booms and crashes.

"Landslide!" I cried, and we fell flat onto the trail as stones large and small smashed their way downslope—beating the earth and whickering through the fog all around us. The rumble became a deafening roar—a cacophony of smashing, splintering rock—and the slope shook, as if the mountain were alive. I opened my eyes in time to see a shattered tree spin lazily past, propeller-like through the mist. I waited—there was nothing else to do—heart skittering, keenly aware that at any second, we might be maimed. Killed. The whole of the slope was in motion, and we were at ground zero.

****

The slide subsided, the roar diminished, and dust

and debris rained gently down, ticking and clicking against the rocks and trees, coating our bodies and packs. From far below came the booming echoes of the final wave of boulders, settling at last.

"You guys okay?" I asked, shaking dust from my hair. Wiping it from my eyes. I got to my knees and discovered I was trembling, head to toe.

"I'm good," Katherine said with a laugh. "Aside from the minor heart attack. That was unbelievable."

"I'm fine," said Heidi.

Dirt rained from her hair as she got to her feet.

"We should keep going," she said, as if we'd just stopped for a snack or to look at the view.

I regarded my companions with a mix of shock and admiration. They seemed so relaxed. So cool.

"You want to keep going after *that*?" I asked.

"Of course," said Heidi, an edge of irritation now in her voice. "Why not?"

I laughed—my nerves still raw and jangling, my heart still flipping and skipping. "Awesome," I replied. "It's just—I mean, shit, that was a monster slide. A huge slide. Biggest I've ever seen. Most people would be a little rattled. Especially in the fog like this."

Katherine smiled. A gleam in her eyes suggesting exhilaration rather than fear. "Yeah," she said. "I thought we were dead."

Heidi shrugged. "Dude, we're in the mountains. Mountains make their own rules. And anyway, no one's hurt."

"Cool," I replied, determined to match my companions' calm. At least superficially. "Cool. Great. Let's keep going then."

****

The landslide that had just liberated millions of tons of rock had done nothing to dislodge the fog. If anything, the cloud enveloping us was thicker and heavier now than it had been before the slide.

We struggled on up the trace, navigating our way around newly downed trees and fresh rockfall. With the adrenaline rush over, I was suddenly hungry. Thirsty. But despite the new obstacles and the burden of my overloaded pack, it felt good to be moving again. Breathing again.

Shit. This is gonna make a good story. Trevor will never believe it.

I craned my neck, peering uphill, seeking a light at the end of our gray tunnel of fog.

The cloud's gonna break any minute now, I told myself, *and then we'll be above it, in the sunshine, admiring the view.*

But the cloud did not break, no light appeared, and the extreme ascent went on. When I wasn't gasping for breath, I tried joking with my companions—about the fog, the interminable trail, the errant pebble lodged in my boot. Judging from the crisp one-word replies, though, it was obvious they weren't in a bantering mood. So we soldiered on in silence, all business, Heidi leading the way at a pace worthy of a seasoned triathlete.

Into colder, thinner air we climbed now—each new fog-shrouded segment of trail looking much like the last.

And then, all at once, a change. Something different in the mist ahead. A vast shape materializing before us like a ghost ship adrift in an alien sea.

****

The shape clarified, the trail leveled off, and I smiled, relieved to see a familiar landmark.

"All right," I called as we paused before the jutting island of rock. "The boulder I showed you on the map. We're more than halfway to the lake."

"Awesome," said Katherine, putting her hand on the cool stone. "I say we take a breather and look around."

I shrugged my pack to the ground. "Definitely."

Feeling almost weightless without my pack, I stepped to the northern end of the boulder, munching trail mix as I walked. Heidi and Katherine followed. "The trace continues right here," I said. "Another hour or so and we'll be at the lake."

We wandered slowly to the opposite end of the boulder, marveling at our ghostly surroundings. With visibility and sound diminished, the universe had shrunk to this single location—a tiny island of solid earth in an ocean of curling mist.

"According to Muir's map," I said as we neared the southern end of the boulder, "the mystery trail begins somewhere over here. Though, like I told you, my dad and brother and I never saw any sign of ..."

I froze.

Before us lay one of the most beautiful paths I'd ever seen—a tightly constructed, carefully engineered lane with broad stone steps and neat retaining walls of meticulously fitted basalt. The path zigzagged up the precipitous slope like a road to a forgotten kingdom.

"This must be new," I mumbled.

But the trail didn't look new. It looked ancient. Like part of the mountain. A geological feature. With steps smoothed and polished—as if by the passage of a million feet. With masonry so old and settled that the bricks appeared fused. Like stonework in a Mayan temple or a Roman amphitheater.

I looked at the boulder again, convinced I'd made a mistake. That the boulder was not the one I'd identified on the map. Not the one I remembered. That we'd somehow lost our way in the mist and climbed to a different location.

There was no mistake. The boulder was the one I'd visited with Trevor and our dad. The very same. No doubt about it. The boulder was distinctive. Unique. With a deep, cave-like cleft along its northern edge. I remembered it clearly.

But I had no recollection of this trail. None whatsoever.

I tried to recall details of the trip with my dad and brother. *How could we have missed this? Is it possible we never walked to this end of the stone?*

"Maybe this trail was overgrown when you were here before," suggested Katherine, as if reading my thoughts. "Maybe the park service restored it. I know they have volunteer crews that do that kind of thing."

"Yeah, that must be it," I mumbled. I didn't believe the explanation. It didn't add up. But I couldn't think of a better one.

Heidi studied the path intently and peered upslope. "Muir's trail," she said matter-of-factly. "And look. The sun's coming out."

It was true. High overhead, there was now an opening in the cloud. A remote window of blue sky illuminating lofty meadows. Above the meadows, jagged snow-covered peaks sparkling in the sun. We gazed up at the light like prisoners at the bottom of a well.

"I don't have a map for this trail," I said softly. "I don't know what's up there."

"So let's find out," said Heidi. Her eyes were shining.

****

As we ate lunch beside the boulder, I studied the Green Trails map—a 1:69,500-scale topographic representation of the quadrant we were in, printed the previous year. Easy to read and rich in detail, it showed rivers, streams, peaks, and valleys. It showed access roads, dead-end logging tracks, and virtually every trail. The trail before us was beautifully made and well maintained, but as far as this map was concerned, it did not exist.

Furthermore—from what I could make of the contour lines on the map—there was no obvious destination for it to climb to. No blue cirque like Torch Lake. No famous glacier or important mountain pass. According to the map, the territory above was brutally steep and rugged, with no place to pitch a tent.

Having divined as much as I could from the map, I turned to my Garmin GPS, but it proved unhelpful, as well. The phrase "Locating Satellite" blinked on the unit's tiny black-and-white screen and stayed there— blink, blink, blink—no matter where I stood or how I pointed the device.

I tried changing the batteries. Still no signal. I'd never heard of fog or cloud cover affecting a GPS, but I couldn't think of another explanation.

I told Heidi and Katherine that if we took this unknown, unnamed route, we'd miss out on Torch Lake. That we couldn't do both. That a traverse across the high country would almost certainly be too difficult. My companions didn't seem to care. They still sounded eager to explore the new trail.

Looking back, I know that "eager" is too mild a term. If I hadn't agreed to the mystery trail, they would have insisted. But I *did* agree. Truth be told, I was curious as hell.

And curiosity was only part of it. Though I'd never seen the trail before—I was positive of that—it was somehow familiar. Ascending elegantly into the fog in front of my eyes, it reminded me of something. Conjured a fragment of a half-remembered dream. I stood there, nerves alight with exultation and terror, knowing that I *had* to feel the strange trail beneath my feet. Had to follow it into the unknown.

We filled our water bottles with clear, icy runoff from a cascading streamlet on the slope above the boulder. And then we were moving again, up the new trail—Heidi in the lead, Katherine in the middle, me in the back.

At the first switchback, I gazed skyward and discovered that the window of light was still there—an aperture of blue framed by jagged snow-blanketed peaks that resembled the razor-edged teeth of a trap.

****

The fog thinned as we climbed, then disintegrated into wispy tatters, and all at once, we were above the vast cloud, walking in full, blazing afternoon sunshine, traversing broad basalt and limestone-choked scree fields and nearly vertical glades of stunted subalpine fir and mountain hemlock. I wanted to pause and celebrate the sunshine and our successful passage through the fog. But my companions pressed on in silence as if nothing had changed.

The scrubby trees gave way to heath shrub meadows of huckleberry and heather. Hawks and golden eagles wheeled overhead, and marmots whistled warnings of our approach before vanishing into sprawling earthen dens.

In the arms of the mountains, in the crisper, cooler air, our shadows lengthened, and I focused on little things. Immediate concerns. Thirst. Hunger. Fatigue. My aching quads, back, and shoulders.

When I lifted my head to look around, I saw new peaks and waterfalls, vast alpine terraces I didn't recognize, and a trail—our trail—leading to a destination I still couldn't discern. I focused on the ascent, fell into a rhythm, a trance, and forced myself to ignore the nagging voice in the back of my brain. The voice telling me that we'd climbed too high, that the position of the sun wasn't right, that there was something wrong with the alignment and attitude of the broad fog-shrouded valley below.

I ignored the voice because it wasn't making sense. Because its warnings couldn't be correct.

****

The serpentine trail opened at last onto a broad, level bench—the only flat patch of ground we'd seen for the past ninety minutes—and we paused together in silence. Doubts and worries notwithstanding, the view from the bench was spectacular.

"What a gorgeous spot," I said, "and there's water."

A cataract of clear, icy snowmelt tumbled noisily through a rocky chute fifty or so yards from the bench. "We should camp here," I said.

To my surprise, my companions agreed.

"Yeah," said Heidi. "This is perfect."

"I love it," said Katherine. "And I'm starving."

We began unloading our packs and setting up our tents, and I studied our surroundings as I worked—the broad, steep scree fields fanning down all around us. The spires of jagged rock far above. The wide cloud-enveloped valley below. A pair of hawks plummeted through the open sky, swooping near the cloud but never venturing inside.

The views were stunning. Jaw-dropping. But some of the things I observed only added to the vague back-of-the-mind disquiet I'd been feeling for hours.

For one thing, Ranger Peak—a hulking flat-topped mountain near the trailhead where we'd left the car—looked too far away. I couldn't reconcile what I was seeing. The distinctive peak looked small and remote, as if we were twenty miles removed from it instead of the seven or eight we'd actually hiked. There was an odd shimmer around the summit, as well, as if I were viewing it through a heat haze or a sheet of antique leaded glass. The distant peak floated above the fog. A lonely atoll in a flat gray sea.

The view uphill was equally unsettling. Our trail did indeed lead to a pass, and a dramatic one at that. I stared at it for a long while, as late afternoon shadow crept across the heights, consuming the mountain inch by inch. Not all of the trail above was visible, but from what I could see, it appeared to ascend to a broad, treeless saddle between two snowy, knife-edged peaks.

The peaks remained in full sun for now—dazzling white spires against a fathomless blue sky. So bright were they that I had to look away.

Lowering my gaze slightly, I saw an unexpected shape at the extreme western edge of the saddle. *A trick of the light. An illusion.*

It looked like the corner of a building. A sliver of a foundation. But it couldn't be. *If there were a ranger cabin or shelter there, it would surely be on the map. Or at least on Google Earth.* I'd studied the maps— paper and Internet versions alike. Read the hiking blogs. Scoured the national park website. The things I was seeing—the trail, the structure—didn't exist. And yet clearly they did.

I decided then that we had indeed gotten way off track in the fog. That the boulder we'd stopped at earlier wasn't the same one I remembered after all. It was the only rational explanation I could think of.

We got off track, and now we're in a different part of the valley. A part I'm unfamiliar with. No harm done. We're not lost. The valley's still there. Ranger Peak is still there—farther away than I'd expect, but still there. We'll find our way back. Relax, I told myself. *Enjoy the view.*

I checked the GPS again. The same unsatisfying message blinked on screen. "Locating Satellite." Blink, blink, blink. Over and over again.

I positioned the device on a rock and willed it to get its shit together as I unpacked the stove. It didn't. The satellite remained "unlocated." Clearly the GPS was broken.

My irritation increased as I checked my altimeter watch and observed our supposed elevation: 8,241 feet.

The watch is broken, too. What the hell is going on? I tapped it. Shook it. Looked again. 8,241 feet. Which was impossible. The highest peak in the entire region—Mount Olympus—is only 7,979 feet. My watch had always been a remarkably accurate and reliable tool, and I couldn't imagine what was wrong with it. Low battery, perhaps? A moot point since I didn't have a spare. *Great.*

Looking back, I realize the thing that disturbed me most about the malfunctioning watch was that deep down, I agreed with the number on the display.

I knew intellectually that we couldn't be at 8,241 feet, but my body said we were. Our perch *felt* that high. It *felt* like we'd climbed long enough and hard enough to attain such an altitude. I didn't process the thought at the time because it was ridiculous, but it's what I believed.

The shadows lengthened, my weariness and appetite increased, and I shoved the concerning thoughts aside and told myself everything would make more sense in the morning. *We're in a safe place, in gorgeous wilderness, with plenty of food and water. And my companions are beautiful and adventurous.*

Heidi was fiddling with her pack, organizing gear. Katherine was inside the tent, changing clothes, almost completely undressed, separated from the outside world only by a sheer veil of mosquito netting. She could've zipped shut the outer opaque door of the tent, but she hadn't done so. And though I didn't gawk, a quick glimpse was enough to take my breath away. Smooth skin. Abundant curves. Toned muscles. Long, flowing hair.

She tugged a fleece jacket on over her head, shook her hair free, and looked right at me. Smiled and winked. I smiled back and forgot my worries completely.

****

The backpacking stove purred, heating a liter of icy mountain stream water for a second batch of whiskey tea. We lay on the grass next to our tents—Heidi and Katherine and I—laughing and talking softly, looking out at the valley as twilight deepened and the sky over the eastern mountains darkened enough to reveal planets glittering like diamonds.

Summer or not, we were bundled in fleece and wool. The temperature had fallen with the fading light, and chill air was wafting up from the fog far below. The fog, stagnant and unchanging, seemed to have settled permanently over the broad valley. But there were no bugs, which was a blessing.

Also, despite the chill, we were warm. We had the proper gear and had eaten well and abundantly. Piping hot spaghetti—the finest in freeze-dried backpacking fare—trail mix, and dark chocolate. Now the whiskey tea was adding to our contentedness.

I told my companions about other trips I'd taken into the Olympic Mountains. About what the wilderness meant to me.

"You really love it out here, don't you, Jake?" Katherine said, in a tone that struck me as wistful. Almost sad.

I replied that I did. And I recited a John Muir quote from memory, explaining that it summed up how I was feeling. "Climb the mountains and get their good tidings. Nature's peace will flow into you as sunshine flows into trees. The winds will blow their own freshness into you, and the storms their energy, while cares will drop off like autumn leaves."

My companions made no reply.

I lay there, feeling serene and relaxed. The whiskey—along with the endorphin buzz I was feeling after the long climb—had put me in a mellow, Zen-like mood. My mind drifted pleasantly.

We'll watch the stars come out and then maybe play cards in one of the tents. Gin rummy, followed by strip poker.

The daydream ended abruptly when the ground trembled and a distant rumble—somewhere beyond the mysterious pass—broke the quiet. Another slide, I guessed. Noteworthy but not alarming, because it was so far away.

I got to my feet and looked toward the pass as the distant tumult continued.

The light was nearly gone, but my eyes had adjusted to the dim conditions. If not for that, I doubt I would've seen the shapes gliding downhill a couple hundred yards away. Gray and ghostlike, moving quickly, silently—barely discernible in the gloom. *Wolves on the hunt. Or coyotes.*

I whispered to Heidi and Katherine, but they said they couldn't see anything. Within seconds, I lost the shapes, as well.

The distant rumble died at last. Silence returned.

Then, a new distraction.

Light.

Firelight.

Perhaps a thousand feet downhill. A campfire flickering, growing stronger.

"Looks like we have company," I said.

Heidi went to her pack and came back with binoculars. Pointed them at the fire and adjusted the focus. "Trevor," she said after a few seconds.

"What?" I replied. "Seriously?"

The thought that my brother had returned filled me with joy. I reached for Heidi's binoculars. A green glow emanated from the lenses. *Night vision. Why does she have night-vision binoculars?*

She handed me the binoculars reluctantly, and I brought them to my eyes.

It took a moment for my brain to adapt to the view. Through the binoculars, everything was a shimmering, phosphorescent green—rocks, trees, trail. But it was Trevor—no doubt about that. He was camped on a narrow, uneven strip of ground just off the path, tent and cooking gear arrayed around him. He was sitting on his pack, making dinner. The fog was just below him—maybe a couple hundred feet—making it appear that he was floating on a cloud.

I smiled, happy to see him, thinking how great it would be to get his take on the strange, unmapped route. And on the other anomalies I'd noticed. As for our earlier argument, it was history as far as I was concerned. In the past. A subject for jokes and future brotherly insults.

"I bet he doesn't even know we're here," said Katherine.

"I bet you're right," I replied. "We're far enough apart—and I think he just set up camp."

I was contemplating calling to Trevor or whistling, when I saw him look up suddenly from his fire, then stand quickly and back away.

"What the hell?" I muttered.

"What is it?" Heidi asked, reaching for her binoculars.

I kept the lenses tight against my eyes, heart

pounding. Something was wrong.

Trevor was turning, this way and that, tense and ready, brandishing his pocketknife like a weapon. I had no idea what he was seeing or hearing, but I wished he had a bigger knife. Trevor wasn't afraid of the dark or the wilderness, having grown up in it like me. But something had spooked him badly.

"Jake," said Heidi, reaching for her binoculars again.

I was about to charge downhill when I saw them. Bodies—pale green in the viewfinder—rushing in from all sides of my brother's camp, lunging in from the darkness. Not wolves. These creatures moved on fluttering, tube-like appendages. There were bright flashes. Blades? Teeth? Trevor twisted and stabbed, kicked and punched—fighting for his life.

The pale-green swarm, now a knot of lithe, sinewy, headless shapes, retreated suddenly, en masse, scurrying from the fire like roaches from a spotlight, leaving Trevor standing alone. I thought for a moment that he had won the fight. Then his limbs jerked, puppet-like, and he convulsed, clawed at his throat, teetered, spun, and dropped face-first onto the trail. Blood pooled around his head.

"Trevor!" I screamed. "Trevor!"

Heidi jerked the binoculars from my hands, but before she did so, I saw several of the pale creatures pivot in our direction.

The sight of the things' fluttering limbs and faceless, eyeless bodies turned my spine to ice.

They stood a moment, staring up at us in the darkness, and then they were moving again. Scurrying uphill. Coming for us.

****

"Shit," said Heidi. "We need to move."

And then we were stumbling in the dark, fumbling with our gear. I'd taken my boots off, and now I jammed them back on my feet and tied them badly, my fingers numb with cold and terror.

I'd had dreams in my life where something or someone was chasing me, where I couldn't get away, where it seemed like my limbs were made of lead. That's how it was on the mountain. Monsters were coming to kill me, and I was moving in slow motion. Constrained. Paralyzed by exhaustion and fear and the shock of seeing my brother die.

Click. Click. Heidi and Katherine were kneeling over plastic cases, hands working fluidly, assembling objects that glinted in the dark.

Then Heidi was on her feet again, swinging her pack onto her back. She held a rifle in one hand.

Heidi has a gun, my dazed brain mused. *Why the hell does Heidi have a gun?*

She moved to the downhill edge of the bench, lifted the weapon to her shoulder, and peered through the scope, which was glowing green like the binoculars. And now Katherine was at her side, holding a rifle of her own, also aiming downhill.

"Jake," Katherine said calmly, without moving, "throw whatever you need in your pack and get ready to run."

A split-second later, Heidi and Katherine fired their rifles. The weapons roared—muzzles flashing in the dark, the shots booming and echoing around the valley. Stone cracked, and voices shrieked and wailed not far below.

I threw a water bottle, a jacket, and a knife into my pack. Lunged through the open door of my tent and groped for my wallet. Realized my headlamp was still on my head and switched it on.

"Turn off the goddamn light," Heidi commanded, firing her rifle as she spoke.

I shut the headlamp off.

"We're not stopping them," Katherine announced flatly. "We need to go."

Then she was moving my way in the darkness, fast but without panic. She grabbed my arm. "Is the journal in your pack?" she said.

"What?"

"Muir's journal. Is it in your pack?"

I stared at her. Numb. Not processing the question. "Trevor's dead," I said. "What *are* those things?"

She grabbed my face with one hand, turned my head so that we were eye to eye, and spoke slowly. Forcefully. "Do. You. Have. The. Journal?"

"Yes. I have the fucking journal. Never took it out of my pack. Why does …?"

"Then let's go."

And then we were running blindly up the trail, stumbling over rocks and roots we couldn't see.

We'd run only a couple hundred yards when we heard shrill, tremulous wailing behind us, followed by the clang and clatter of gear as the swarm overran our camp. Heidi and Katherine spun in unison, and Heidi dropped to one knee. They sighted their rifles again. Fired.

The roar of the guns reverberated around the canyon, bouncing off cliffs and ridges, making two weapons sound like a hundred. The mewling, inhuman voices squealed and caterwauled.

The booming died away, and we were running once more, into blackness.

****

We ascended the trail at an insane pace. My lungs burned. My ears rang. I listened hard for sounds of pursuit but could hear only my own breathing. And my heart thumping like a pile driver.

"What are those things?" I gasped after a few minutes. "And why do you have guns?"

"No talking," Heidi hissed. "Not yet."

We climbed on.

And on.

The events I'd witnessed through Heidi's night-vision binoculars were burned into my mind. The hallucinatory swarm. Trevor fighting for his life. Clutching at his throat. Bleeding to death. I pictured our mom and dad, learning of Trevor's passing. Wondered if I would be the one to deliver the news or if I would die on the mountain, as well.

My boots slipped and slid on my heels, blistering my skin. I wanted to stop and tie them correctly, but our pace would not permit it. My own fear would not permit it. My feet hurt. My legs ached. The only good news was that my pack was far lighter than it had been, due to the fact that I'd left half my gear in the camp.

The camp. Overrun. Ransacked.

I wondered where we would sleep. Where we would be safe.

My tired mind drifted, and I imagined I was participating—unwittingly—in some kind of surreal game.

If that's the case, I reasoned, *then Trevor is still*

alive.

This is all some kind of elaborate play. A performance-art piece no one told me about. The creatures are really just people—actors—wearing makeup.

But I dismissed the thought almost as quickly as it had formed.

I'd seen the attack. Seen the creatures and their faces. They were real. My brother was dead.

****

We topped a rise in the darkness. The trail flattened out abruptly, and we found ourselves on another broad bench—this one still partially full of snow. Water churned through a stony channel somewhere near at hand.

Heidi stopped walking. We all did.

The snow glimmered faintly, reflecting the starlight, and I saw that the bench was backed by a sheer wall of rock. The trail continued via stairs cut into the wall. I wondered how far we were from the pass and the mysterious building I'd seen earlier—if that's indeed what it was.

Heidi stepped to the downhill edge of the bench. Scanned the slope below with her binoculars. Katherine and I waited in the darkness. Breathing. Listening—or trying to listen—over the cacophony of the stream.

"No sign of them," Heidi whispered after several seconds. "Nothing. I think we're in the clear."

Katherine, in the shadows to my right, sighed with relief.

But then there was another sound, barely audible above the rushing water. A faint but solid thump. Then another. And another. Thump. Thump. Thump.

"Shit," Katherine hissed. Then the bench exploded in a rush of noise and movement.

A heavy form smashed Heidi backward, into the snow. The binoculars, glowing green, spun from her hands.

Katherine lifted her rifle. Fired. Hit something inches from my face. Bits of flesh and warm, foul-smelling liquid spattered my head and arms.

Katherine's rifle roared again and again, and in the flashes of the muzzle, I saw shapes flowing over the lip of the bench and dropping from the wall. Thump, thump, thump. The creature's tube-like appendages—glistening and translucent—surged with liquid.

Katherine fired another burst, and then Heidi was shooting again, as well—a handgun this time.

In the dark, amid the blaze of gunfire and the swirl of bodies, time slowed. The battle raged but left me untouched. Unscathed. Like I was a statue in the middle of a war.

I was frozen.

Then everything changed again.

A massive form swept past me in the dark, collided with Katherine, and sent her flying sideways into the cliff face.

Another creature smashed head-on into me. I careened backward to land turtle-like, on my pack, in the snow. The creature—huge and heavy—landed on my chest. I heard a crack, and air blasted from my lungs. The thing's undulating limbs silhouetted against the stars,

The beast pressed against my chest. I writhed. Struggled to pull away.

There was a blinding flash. An eardrum-shattering

boom. Heidi had thrown something—a flash-bang grenade, I later learned—into the center of the swarm. And with a thin, ear-piercing wail, the thing was off me, twisting away into the darkness.

An identical explosion came a moment later, and in the millisecond burst of illumination, I saw that the bench was empty, save for the three of us.

The swarm was gone.

****

In the daylight-bright flash of the grenades, I'd seen Katherine lying inert, face down in the snow at the base of the wall, and I resolved now to go to her. To find her in the darkness. Moving, though, proved exceedingly difficult.

I rolled onto my side, grunting and gasping as bright bolts of pain ricocheted around my chest and back. It hurt to turn. To lift my arms. To breathe. The straps of my backpack dug into my shoulders as I tried to stand, inducing fresh waves of agony. I wondered absently how bad the pain would be later, realizing that I was probably in shock and numb to the full extent of my injuries.

Ears ringing like fire alarms, breath coming in sharp gasps, I stumbled toward the wall, the white-hot afterimage of the grenade flickering in my peripheral vision like an aurora. A million-watt camera flash.

Ten paces. Fifteen. I found Katherine by dead reckoning and knelt beside her, shrugging my pack painfully to the ground.

"Katherine?"

No reply.

I rolled her onto her back and checked for a pulse. She was alive. Breathing. Skin wet with what I guessed was blood.

"Katherine, can you hear me?"

I remembered my headlamp. Found the switch. Flicked it on.

She looked pale and corpse-like, lying there, mouth open, eyes closed, breath coming in shallow, rhythmic hitches. Blood oozed from her nose and from a gash on her neck.

I touched her face and was suddenly aware of another presence in the darkness. Someone standing a few feet away in the snow.

Heidi.

I hadn't heard her approach—not surprising, given the ringing and roaring in my ears.

"She alive?" Heidi asked, without stepping closer.

"Yes," I replied. "But unconscious. I'm guessing she hit her head. Not sure."

I peered at Heidi. Saw the outline of her body against the stars. My vision was coming back. "What about you?" I asked. "You hurt?"

"I'm fine. You?"

"Broken rib. Or ribs. We need to get help."

Heidi said nothing. Just stood there. Silent in the darkness.

"Heidi?"

"You need to stay here," she said at last, as if she'd come to a conclusion about something.

"What do you mean? Stay with Katherine? Where are you going?"

"You can't leave the bench."

"I don't understand."

"The bench should be fine," she said. "It's close enough. But you can't go down. Even if she dies, you can't leave."

"What are you talking about?" I asked, wondering if Heidi had sustained a head injury of her own.

She said nothing. Just stood there, watching me.

"Heidi?"

"Take off your boot," she said. "The right one."

"My boot? Why?"

She crouched beside me. Pointed her handgun at my face. Looped her finger around the trigger. "Do it."

"Heidi, what are you doing? What's going…?"

"The boot!" she screamed. "Now. Before I blow your goddamned head off."

I slid the boot off my right foot, my hands shaking.

"My foot will freeze," I said.

"I'm not going to take your boot," Heidi said mildly as she put down the gun and lifted a grapefruit-sized rock from the snow. With shocking speed and brutality, she smashed the rock down on my stocking foot. Bones crunched and snapped.

"Bitch!" I screamed as fresh pain engulfed me. "Jesus Christ! What the hell's wrong with you?"

And then she was backing away, adjusting her rifle on her shoulder and moving for the stairway in the wall.

"Goodbye, Jake," she said. "This should all be over soon."

****

I screamed Heidi's name again and again, along with a flood of expletives, but there was no reply. Only the crunch of boots on loose gravel above me. The clatter of small stones. The sounds became faint, then disappeared altogether, subsumed by the rush of the stream and the whistle of the breeze against the cliff.

I sat in the snow next to Katherine, consumed by

steady, agonizing pain, and carefully, slowly pulled my boot back onto my foot. The foot was already swollen and throbbing—especially around the arch. Even gently flexing my toes heightened my suffering a hundredfold, and I cursed Heidi's name again. The foot was broken, no doubt about it.

I shivered violently. After the exertion of the hike, the death of my brother, and the adrenaline buzz of the battle, my body was cooling off. Fast. I guessed Katherine was cold, too.

I dug into my pack and found some items I hadn't unpacked at camp. A plastic bag full of hand warmers. A wool hat. Gloves. A tiny stuff sack containing an ultralightweight down jacket. A first-aid kit. An emergency Mylar blanket folded into a tiny stuff sack.

I pulled the jacket on over my fleece—gasping and wincing with every movement—put on the gloves and hat and swallowed four ibuprofens from the first-aid kit. I opened ten of the hand warmers and tucked them into my jacket pockets, my boots, my gloves. I put hand warmers in Katherine's jacket pockets, as well.

I found her hands. They were bare and cold. Exposed on the snow. I bent her arms and tucked her hands into her pockets. She was still unconscious.

Placing my hand under Katherine's neck, I lifted her head as gently as I could and slid my nearly empty pack underneath as a sort of pillow. A barrier between her head and the snow. I unfolded the blanket, shook it out, and tucked it in around us as best I could.

Then I sat and listened for a long time, half expecting to hear the creatures coming back. Or Heidi climbing the slope above me. But there was only the water and the wind.

I scanned the bench with my headlamp. It was empty, save for trampled, bloody snow. There were no bodies. Apparently, the creatures had carried their dead and wounded away in the immediate aftermath of the battle.

Another sweep with the light and I spotted something else. Something partially concealed in the snow about twenty feet away, something that glinted and gleamed in the light. Katherine's rifle.

I got to my feet, gasping through the pain, struggling for breath. It felt as if giant clamps were squeezing my chest, limiting my intake of air.

I took a hobbling old-man step toward the rifle, endeavoring to keep most of my weight on my left foot. It didn't work. The ground was slippery and uneven, and when I did put even a tiny bit of weight on the right foot, it felt like ice picks were being jammed into the arch. Waves of pain lit up my ankle, my calf, my entire lower leg. I cursed Heidi's name again.

I collected the rifle, almost falling on my face in the process, and noticed Katherine's backpack lying a couple of feet farther on. I grabbed it, as well, limped back to where I'd been sitting, and lowered myself into the snow with a grunt. I tucked the blanket back around me, kept the headlamp on, and examined the gun.

I knew a little bit about guns. My dad taught Trevor and me how to shoot when we were young boys. He took us to the range and target-shooting in the woods. He enrolled us in hunter safety courses and showed us how to clean and confidently store weapons and ammunition. The gun I was looking at now was a fully automatic military-style AR-15. Surprisingly lightweight, it appeared undamaged and had a long, curved clip of ammunition that looked to be about three-quarters full. I'd never fired such a weapon but had no doubt I could do so and was glad to have it. I set the gun carefully on the edge of the blanket.

I grabbed Katherine's backpack and emptied it into my lap. Another clip for the AR-15, another first-aid kit, a Nalgene bottle full of water, and several protein bars. From the side pouch tumbled two telescopic hiking poles, collapsed and compact.

I drank half a liter of the water and ate two of the protein bars. I thought about firing three shots from the AR-15—as a distress signal—but dismissed the idea almost as soon as it came to mind. Heidi and Katherine had each fired their rifles at least fifty times during the attack. It had sounded like a war. If there had been rescuers, they would have heard. Also, I didn't want to waste the ammunition. And I worried, perhaps illogically, that a distress signal—any kind of distress signal—might induce the creatures to return.

I lay back, slowly, and rested my head on my pack next to Katherine. Slid closer to her. Stared at the stars and listened to the night. Katherine's breathing had morphed into a thin, irregular wheeze. Not a good sign.

We needed help. Fast. And I had no idea how to make that happen. I tried the sat phone again. Still not working. I resolved to rest for a few minutes and think about the problem. Come up with a plan. A solution.

Instead, almost instantly, I fell asleep.

****

I awoke—I have no idea how much later—to the sound of Katherine's voice.

"Jake? What happened? Jake, wake up."

I opened my eyes. The sky was still dark and full

of stars—though not as many as before.

"Jake?"

"I'm awake," I said, trying to sit up. "Oh, fuck," I gasped and lay immediately back down. The eight hundred milligrams of ibuprofen I'd swallowed earlier had done nothing to mitigate my pain. Every inch of my chest, neck, and back hurt, and my foot and lower leg felt like they were being simultaneously stabbed and crushed in a vise.

I thought about my dead brother and the things he'd said to me on the trail—the comments that had triggered our argument. He'd told me that he didn't trust Heidi and Katherine. That they were up to something. "Yeah," he'd said, "they're beautiful. They're also full of shit. Taking you for a ride, little brother. Though I haven't figured out their game yet."

Trevor's suspicions—so ridiculous-sounding earlier in the trip—were now on a continuous loop in my brain. I wished I'd listened to him.

But wishing wasn't going to change what had happened. Or how I felt.

Powering through my discomfort, groaning and grunting, I sat up all the way and looked around.

The bench was still dark, but to the east, a thin ribbon of light fringed the mountains, casting every craggy peak and weatherworn pass in a soft cerulean glow. Dawn was coming, and even in the sorry state I was in, I noticed the beauty. It was impossible not to.

I peered at Katherine. She hadn't moved and wasn't trying to sit up. It was too dark to see her face.

"How are you feeling?" I asked.

"I've had better days," she said softly.

"Can you sit up?"

"No. I tried. I can't move anything. Jake…?"

"Are you carrying a radio?" I asked. "A sat phone? I didn't see one in your pack."

"I have a sat phone," she said miserably. "In the lower camp. Left it in the tent. Where's Heidi?"

"Gone," I said. "And If I see her again, I'll shoot her."

"What happened?"

"She broke my foot and pretty much left us here to die."

I told Katherine everything that had transpired while she was unconscious.

"I'm sorry Heidi hurt you," she said, after I had finished.

I looked at Katherine, lying there, motionless in the snow. It was still too dark to see her face.

"Who are you?" I asked. "Really. The two of you?"

No reply.

"Why do you have automatic weapons and night-vision gear?"

No response.

"What are those creatures, and why did they attack Trevor?"

"No one was supposed to die," Katherine rasped, her voice barely audible.

She went quiet for a long time. Then, "Is there water? I'm so thirsty."

I uncapped my Nalgene bottle and held it close to her face. She didn't move.

"I can't lift my arms," she whispered, sounding now on the verge of tears.

"I'll help you."

I twisted closer to her, suppressing my own pain,

and held the bottle to her lips. Tilted it gently.

She drank, a lot, and when she spoke again, the rasp was gone, but she still sounded weak. Tired.

"No one was supposed to die," she said again. "We were just supposed to secure the opening. Hold it open until they could make it permanent."

"What are you talking about? What opening? And who's 'they'?"

Katherine fell silent again. When she spoke this time, there was resignation in her voice—as if she'd weighed her options and decided to tell me the truth. As if there was nothing to lose.

"Jake," she said quietly. "Muir's journal—you said you inherited it, right?"

"Yeah. It was my grandfather's. My dad found it in his house last year, after he died. No one in the family knew he had it. Or how he came by it."

"I do," said Katherine. "We put it there."

"What?"

"Not me personally but the people I work for."

"Why?"

"We needed you to have it. You, specifically. We figured your dad would give it to you. Because of your love of the Olympics. All the hiking you do."

"You broke into my grandfather's house?"

"We needed you to have the journal. Needed you to open it. Read it. Absorb it. Decide for yourself to look for the mystery trail. We needed it to be *your* idea. We thought that might affect the odds. Make the opening more likely to occur."

I wondered for a moment if Katherine was talking in her sleep. "Katherine …?"

"You have a talent, Jake. A very special talent.

Though you don't realize it."

"Talent?" I said skeptically.

"A gene. Extremely rare. Based on the research my employer has conducted, fewer than one in a billion people have it."

I said nothing.

"Muir had it—we know that from testing one of his hair samples. I'm sure there were others before him.

"Among living people, there's a woman in Ethiopia. An old man in southern Australia. A toddler in Madrid. A death row prisoner in Iran. And you. That's it, as far as we know, from checking and cross-checking global databases. There might be others. A handful. In the whole world."

I didn't know what to say. Her words made little sense, and the pain in my foot and chest was making it hard to think.

I focused on the water churning through the narrow defile. The wind intermittently gusting against the cliff. The light growing—giving shape and form to the slopes on either side of us and the icy summits above, erasing the shadows, one by one. The sea of fog was still there, 1,500 feet below us, a vast white cloud. But there were holes in the blanket now. Perforations, like windows, revealing bits of forest and meadow on the valley floor.

I looked once more at Katherine—gritting my teeth through the pain—and nearly recoiled at the sight of her. In the thin light, she looked pallid, jaundiced, and frail. Like a hospice patient in the final moments of life. The vibrant, healthy young woman I'd hiked with the previous day was no more, and a wave of compassion overrode my anger and fear.

"You don't have any idea what I'm talking about,

do you?" she whispered.

"No," I replied. "I'm sorry. I don't."

Her gaze flicked to the cliff above us, then to the strange pass high above that. The way Heidi had gone a few hours earlier.

"The slope we're on," said Katherine, "this mountain, the pass up there, the valley on the other side—they exist, obviously. They're real. But they're closed to virtually everyone—except people like you."

I said nothing.

"Imagine owning an old mansion," said Katherine, "living there for years, and then suddenly discovering a room between some walls. A sealed room. A room you didn't even know existed. That's how they explained it to us in one of the briefings."

"Who's 'they'?"

Katherine coughed, and I lifted the water bottle to her mouth again. She took a sip.

"The company. They hired us. Gave a briefing. Asked us to connect with you. Bring you out here."

"*Bring* me here?" I said. "I invited you, remember?"

"Yes. That's how it was supposed to go down. Like it was all your idea. We figured you'd talk about Muir's journal online, and you did. We connected with you then. Told you we liked hiking, that we were looking for an adventure."

I thought about it. Realized she was right. They'd both friended me on Facebook—immediately after I posted about Muir's journal. They'd made the initial contact.

"You're telling me the trail we hiked yesterday," I said, "the mystery trail, wouldn't … what? Be visible if

I wasn't here?"

"Correct."

She paused as if to catch her breath. I waited. Studied the sky.

"Your presence here," she continued, "changes everything. Reveals things we wouldn't otherwise see. Opens the door, so to speak, and keeps it open—as long as you stay in the vicinity."

"But I've been out here before," I said. "Lots of times. I never saw anything unusual."

Katherine smiled feebly. "Yes, but you weren't *looking* for anything those other times. And you didn't have Muir's journal. The people who hired us said you've probably triggered openings in the past—here and there. Witnessed anomalies without even knowing they *were* anomalies. The lands blend seamlessly together after all. You wouldn't necessarily know you'd crossed a line. Not at first, anyway."

I made no reply.

"You think I'm crazy," said Katherine, "or full of shit, right?"

I shrugged.

"I know how it sounds, Jake. But think about what's happened. And the things we've seen. A long, elaborately built trail that's not on any maps—that doesn't even show up on Google Earth. Malfunctioning gear. Unnamed peaks taller than anything else nearby. The creatures—whatever they are."

I laughed bitterly. "The company didn't tell you about the creatures? Nice of them."

Katherine coughed. "They said there would be aberrations, things they couldn't anticipate. Possibly other life forms—but nothing specific."

I shook my head. "You say Muir had this ... ability, or talent, or whatever it is. Why would someone even suspect that? Because of his journal? The guy's been dead for over a hundred years."

Katherine shivered, and I tucked the Mylar blanket in tighter around her.

"Remember the notation we read in the journal?" she said. "Below the map, at the bottom of the page—about Muir's meeting with Roosevelt?"

"Yeah?"

"Muir was upset that someone else was at the meeting, remember?"

I nodded. "Luther Holloway. The timber guy."

Katherine coughed. "Right. Muir hated Holloway, but there wasn't much he could do about his presence at meetings because important people in Roosevelt's administration wanted him there. Friends in high places, you know?"

"I guess."

"After Muir discovered the mystery trail and where it leads, he went straight to Roosevelt to describe what he'd seen and ask that the entire Olympic ecosystem be protected. As a sanctuary. A national park. Holloway was at that meeting.

"Roosevelt was conservation-minded and inclined to agree with Muir, but Muir's description of this particular place—especially Strath ay Banrigh, as he called it—was so extraordinary, so over the top that Roosevelt insisted on seeing it for himself."

I listened, staring out at the alpine wonderland around us.

"They arranged a trip," she said, "and a presidential entourage traveled here, on horseback."

I made no reply.

"They kept it quiet—per Muir's request. Or as quiet as they could. Muir was worried about outsiders getting wind of what he'd discovered.

"Unfortunately, Holloway saw everything."

I looked around at the bench. The slope. The jagged, impassive peaks above. "You're saying Roosevelt climbed this trail?"

Katherine nodded. "Yes. They all did. And it amazed them to no end."

She glanced at me. Then her gaze drifted once more toward the pass, and she continued softly. "But after they crossed the pass and descended into the valley on the other side … after they saw what was there … well, the trail seemed like nothing. It was forgotten."

"What's on the other side?" I asked.

Katherine's eyes clouded, and she continued in a voice tinged with sadness. "A valley," she whispered. "Like I said."

She hesitated and looked away.

"A *hallowed* valley. Broad and fertile and different from any other place on the planet. The trees there grow larger than redwoods. Larger than any trees anywhere—according to the company. Wildlife is plentiful, and the streams run fast and cold and clear. And there's a lake. Pristine. Shimmering. Sacred. A jewel in the center of a crown."

"You keep saying 'the company,'" I said. "*What* company?"

"Greenfield. That's who hired us."

"I've heard of it. I think."

"It's a 75-billion-dollar multinational, founded a

hundred years ago by a man named Luther Holloway, the great-grandfather of the current chairman."

I stared at her. "Holloway?"

"Yes, he …" Katherine gagged, wheezing and convulsing as if she were choking on a piece of steak.

I did my best to comfort her, but the fit went on for a long time. When she continued at last, her voice was a strained whisper.

"Holloway," she said, "started the company after Roosevelt left office and built it into a timber and mining empire. He was a shrewd businessman. Ambitious. Ruthless. Obsessed. Most of all … obsessed."

"With what?"

"Strath ay Banrigh," Katherine said, as if the answer were obvious. "The Valley of the Queen.

"Holloway brought surveyors out here in 1905, intending to enter the valley again. Map it. Catalog it. Come up with a plan to log it—legally or illegally.

"But he couldn't find the trail because Muir wasn't with him.

"Holloway thought he'd somehow entered the wrong drainage and tried again. And again. He sent crews up the adjacent river valleys and eventually to every corner of the range. They found nothing.

"Years passed. The people close to Holloway assumed he'd given up his weird quest—but it was not so. He'd simply changed focus. Instead of scouring the Olympics over and over, he shifted his attention to Muir.

"He'd heard rumors about Muir's strange talents years earlier and had disbelieved them out of hand. Holloway was a pragmatic, unimaginative man. But after a time, he came around.

"He'd seen Strath ay Banrigh with his own eyes—the impossibly tall trees, the gold in the streams—and he couldn't get it out of his mind.

"He built a special room at corporate headquarters. A locked and guarded room devoted to the study of the mysterious valley. He gathered every scrap of information he could. He appropriated Muir's journals—legally and otherwise. He hired scientists. Let his family and a few chosen board members in on the secret."

I made no reply.

"It's likely he wouldn't have been able to convince them, except for one thing."

Katherine paused as if she needed to rest. As if simply telling the story was wearing her out.

The upper mountain was in full sun now, and soon the bench would be, as well.

"Holloway," Katherine said at last, "had photographs. Images from his trip with Muir and Roosevelt. Pictures of peaks and passes, trees and trails that no one could identify or explain.

"But even with the photographs, some—or maybe even most—of Holloway's heirs thought the old man was crazy. Imagined he had somehow doctored the images and fabricated the story for some unknown motive.

"Still, they kept the secret room intact—out of tradition or a sense family obligation, I don't know—but nothing much happened after Holloway's passing. Not until a few years ago, when the current chairman decided to try a new approach."

"DNA analysis," I said.

"Right. He created a special team. Put some money behind it. A lot of money. Set some goals. The team researched the entire story again exhaustively and got hold of a piece of Muir's DNA. They ran a bunch of tests and found the anomaly." She looked at me. "The 'portal gene.'"

I made no reply. Even after everything that had happened, I still couldn't believe what she was saying.

"And then," Katherine continued, "they went looking for the same marker among the general population. And they found you."

Wind whistled over the bench. A lonely, desolate sound.

"How could you agree to such a thing?" I said.

"I never imagined it would turn out like this."

"My brother is dead."

Her eyes filled with tears, but she said nothing further.

"Great," I said. "So now what happens? What's the company's plan? Leave us here to die of exposure?"

"No." Katherine replied. "They're on their way."

"Who is?"

"The company. Jake, don't you see?"

I shook my head. "No. I don't."

"As long as you're here, on this bench, the trail stays open. In fact, the longer you stay here, on this bench, in this transition zone—the more fixed the opening becomes. Soon the hidden lands will be a permanent part of the landscape. Open to everyone. In a few hours, this will all be visible from the air. From satellites.

"The company has been massing equipment at a staging area. Heavy machinery. Helicopters. Men. They started preparing weeks ago—after they determined their plan might actually work. They intend to act before anyone else realizes what's going on. They plan to get to the valley first."

"To do what?" I asked. "Cut the trees? Get the gold?"

"Yes, all of that."

She blinked more tears away. "And much more. Much worse."

I stared at her, and the memory of a recent dream flashed in my brain. Just a fragment. A freeze-frame.

In the dream I was looking at a meadow from high overhead. A lush, serene place. There was a lake at one end of the meadow and an enormous rock at the other, big as a mansion and cracked in the middle, as if split asunder by some giant's hammer.

I was certain there was more to the dream. I could *feel* it. But try as I might, I could remember nothing further. Nor could I say why Katherine's words had brought the dream to mind. Yet the memory was deeply troubling.

Katherine stared helplessly at the sky. Her skin was deathly pale.

"Katherine," I said gently. "What is the company planning to do?"

No response.

A feeling of inexplicable dread swelled in my mind.

"Where did Heidi go?" I asked.

No answer.

"Katherine, tell me what's going on."

Her reply came in a tight, ragged whisper. "They think that if they kill her, everything will be easier."

"Kill who?"

My heart thumped with a wave of fresh panic. *The dream. There was a woman in the dream.*

"We're tied to her," said Katherine. "They know that. They know we need her. They think if they break the connection …"

"Kill who?" I asked again. "And where did Heidi go?"

"It's not just the company," she said, her voice so faint now that I had to lean close to her lips to hear. "A lot of people want her dead."

Katherine's eyes snapped suddenly wide, and her face twisted into a mask of pain. She coughed and choked, spitting up bright rivulets of bloody phlegm.

I held her. Stroked her hair. "Katherine …"

"You have to find Heidi, Jake. You have to stop her."

****

I held Katherine until her convulsions stopped. Until the anguish disappeared from her face, her mouth went slack, and the rise and fall of her chest ceased. Her eyes remained open, staring, in death, but I closed them.

In pain, full of despair, I tried to make sense of the situation. The dark dream that had resurfaced from my subconscious lingered and churned, a rumor growing louder.

A mirror-bright flash far down-valley—near Ranger Peak—caught my eye. The flash was much too distant to identify, but I knew in my gut what I was looking at. The machines Katherine had spoken of—Greenfield's logging and road-building equipment, massing in a staging area. I pictured backhoes and bulldozers, front loaders and enormous helicopters capable of carrying such machines, in a vast dirt clearing—clouds of dust swirling in the air, people hustling about, supervisors barking orders. An army preparing for battle.

They're on their way.

****

I don't know if the decision I came to then was rational or not. But I made up my mind quickly.

I will climb to the pass. I will descend into the valley. I will stop Heidi.

Stop her from what, I did not know.

If you'd asked me then to explain myself, I couldn't have done so. But the thought of staying on the bench and waiting for "the company" to arrive was intolerable.

I believed the things Katherine had told me, at last. Outlandish as it all seemed, I believed her. The staggeringly tall peaks, the strange trail, and the bizarre events I'd witnessed made it difficult *not* to believe. There was, too, my own sense of dread, triggered by the dream, growing stronger by the minute.

****

I put the AR-15 inside my pack, with the muzzle and eight inches of barrel protruding from the top. I considered carrying the rifle in my hand or slinging it over my shoulder—but given my injuries, I wanted my hands free and unencumbered.

To my pack I added Katherine's first-aid kit, a full water bottle, some energy bars, and an extra ammunition clip. Her first-aid kit contained Vicodin, I discovered, and I was tempted to swallow a couple on the spot but decided against it. The trail above was narrow and steep, and I had no idea what I would encounter at the pass and beyond. I needed to stay sharp.

I laced my hiking boots, taking great care with my injured foot. The foot throbbed painfully, rhythmically and felt like it had swelled to twice its normal size. Even gentle pressure on the laces made me want to howl, and the idea of walking anywhere seemed impossible, absurd. Still, I was determined to try.

I extended Katherine's hiking poles and leveraged myself into a standing position. Doing so took pressure off my injured foot—that was the good news—but it spawned searing jolts of pain in my chest and back.

I stood there in the snow, gasping, looking around. A very different man from the one who'd started up the mountain the previous day.

Far below, the sea of fog was breaking up, revealing more of the valley floor. The river.

I could see nothing of the trail we'd hiked.

I faced the cleft in the wall, where the stairs began. Took one small, tentative, wobbling step. Then another, putting as much weight as possible on the poles, using them like crutches.

Grunting and groaning, I began to climb.

****

The ascent to the pass was a pilgrimage of pain, breathtaking and unrelenting. The hurt in my foot was more intense than in my chest and back, and just when I thought I could endure it no longer, the appendage went numb. I pictured my toes turning black and gangrenous inside the boot. Imagined the foot slick and hideously swollen, ready to burst. I envisioned a doctor regretfully explaining that amputation was the only option.

But I didn't stop to examine the foot. There was nothing I could do about it anyway. I hobbled on, stepping as gingerly as possible.

How long the trip took I cannot say. Three hours? Four? That part of the journey is a blur. A vaguely remembered exercise in suffering. One small, teetering step after another.

At last, I topped a rise, and the pass unfolded before me, a broad, barren saddle worn smooth by wind and ice and time. The shape I'd seen from far below was indeed the corner of a cabin. Solid and rough-hewn and so worn and settled that it looked like it might have been there for a thousand years.

It was hard to tell for sure because the structure was on fire.

****

I wondered at first if Heidi had set the fire, or perhaps the creatures that had attacked us in the night. Or maybe it was the old man sitting on a rock nearby.

He was about one hundred feet from the cabin, staring into the conflagration with a look of grim determination.

Resolute and immovable, the old man seemed. Like a statue. And yet there was a fragility about him also, which suggested that his determination might not last. That he might soon break under the weight of his burden—whatever that was.

I approached him from the side, seeing only his profile, for he did not turn or lift his gaze from the fire.

When he looked up at last, I gasped. The right side of his ancient, weather-beaten face was torn and bloody. An oozing three-inch gash beneath his right eye shone orange in the firelight, and the eye itself was swollen shut, the lid purple and black. There were cuts on his scalp, too, and blood caked in his wild gray hair. He got to his feet and watched me approach, saying nothing.

"Are you okay?" I asked, tottering forward, leaning heavily on my hiking poles.

He stared at me with his good eye but made no reply.

I hobbled close, and he reached for my hand. He took it as soon as I let go of the hiking pole, squeezing it in both of his hands. They were rough. Gnarled. Surprisingly strong. His clothing was the color of the surrounding soil and looked handmade.

"What happened?" I asked.

No answer. No utterance of any kind. Just his eye searching my eyes. Studying my face with an urgency and intensity I could feel. His damaged eye fluttered and twitched beneath its bruised, mutilated lid, struggling to open.

"Were you attacked?" I asked. "Do you have a satellite phone? We need to get help."

No response. Just staring. Probing. Yet I sensed a keen intelligence in the old man's wizened visage. And kindness also. Compassion. Something else, as well— profound despair.

"What happened?" I asked again as the fire raged behind us.

Ancient timbers popped and cracked, and a section of roof collapsed, sending up a fountain of sparks.

The old man clutched my hand more tightly. Held my gaze. I wondered, absently, illogically, if he was reading my mind. Or inviting me to read his.

I felt the strength in his grip diminish ever so

slightly, and then I saw it—blood soaking his shirt, flowing from some massive wound on his side.

"You need to sit down," I said. "I need to see to your injuries."

The old man blinked, and I imagined that he might pass out. That I might have to catch him—no easy feat, given my pathetic condition.

I heard—or felt—a click in my mind, like a key turning in a lock, and then it was I who lost consciousness.

****

When I awoke, or came to, I was alone and walking rapidly downhill through a grove of enormous, ancient trees. I was still wearing my pack and my tattered, bloodstained clothes, still using hiking poles, but my pain was gone. Completely gone.

I took a long stride. Put all my weight on my right foot.

No pain.

I flexed my shoulders. Inhaled deeply.

No pain.

I marveled at the miracle of my recovery. Wanted to stop and analyze it but did not. It seemed that my body somehow knew what had happened and where it was going and was waiting for my brain to catch up.

I kept walking, down and down, as strange thoughts and unfamiliar memories unfurled in my mind.

Gradually, bit by bit, illumination came. But before that, and with it, unease. Disquiet.

The despair was nameless at first.

Was the insight and understanding blossoming in my mind a gift from the old man? I wasn't sure. I only knew that the more I comprehended, the more afraid I

159

became.

****

Biologists say that after wolves were reintroduced into Yellowstone National Park, the health of the streams and rivers improved. The connection is not immediately obvious, but it turns out that wolves—restored to their proper place in the ecosystem—culled bloated populations of deer, elk, and moose that had been overgrazing the willows along the stream banks. With the wolves firmly in charge, plant communities recovered. Shade increased, stream temperatures fell, water quality improved, and fish populations rebounded.

Biologists call the phenomenon a "trophic cascade." The loss of a key species in an ecosystem has an effect on everything else. When the wolves were hunted to extinction in Yellowstone, the system unraveled. When they came back, the system began to heal.

As I walked through the silent forest, I understood that the same thing was happening around me. The system here was unraveling—had been unraveling since the previous day, when I unknowingly opened the way to a sacred valley.

Only here, the effect wouldn't be limited to the valley, because the valley was different. Special. What was happening around me was on a different order of magnitude entirely. The unraveling happening here would change the entire planet.

****

Another memory sprang to mind, vivid and bright, like a dream suddenly recalled. *Did this really happen?* I wondered. I wasn't sure.

In the dream, or memory, the old man stood with his back to me, watching the burning cabin.

"She is vulnerable now," he said. "All of creation senses it." He laughed. "Well, *almost* all of creation. One species remains oblivious, but not for much longer."

"Who is vulnerable?" I asked.

"Balance is gone," he said, "and the beasts roam free. Uncontrolled. No wolves to keep them in check."

I knew somehow that he didn't literally mean "wolves" but some other kind of predator—something unique to the valley. By "beasts," I supposed he meant the creatures that had killed my brother. *The beasts roam free ...*

"*Who* is vulnerable?" I asked again, trying to focus on one mystery at a time.

"You opened the way and called to her," he said, "though unknowingly. And she will come—because that is the way of things. And she will die. In that form, she will die easily."

"*Who* will die?" I asked to the old man's back.

He never looked at me. Just stared at the conflagration. The heat from the blaze was almost too much to tolerate. I stood there sweating, eyes watering.

"When I was a boy," said the old man, his voice a morose whisper now, barely audible above the roar of the fire, "I was taught that she believes our destinies are intertwined. That she sees something in us—a hint of what we might become."

Another section of roof collapsed. I took a step back, away from the heat, but the old man never moved.

"But I think she's wrong," he said. "I think we're

destined to go our own way. To our undoing."

****

I hiked on, trying desperately to recall other fragments, other thoughts. A thousand questions swirled in my mind.

A thousand riddles.

Descending quickly and steadily now, I entered a grove of spectacularly large trees. It was quiet inside the majestic grove—there was no sound but my footsteps—and darker. But there was a window of light far ahead. An opening.

Under different circumstances, I certainly would have stopped to study the giants around me. Trees with trunks as big around as houses. But now I hurried on, through the gloom, toward the light, the sunshine—turning a copper color now as afternoon became evening—knowing that I was meant to go there, even as my rational, conscious mind struggled to understand.

Looking back, I realize I couldn't bear to contemplate the trees just then, knowing that someone intended to cut them all. The trees around me had survived for centuries, maybe a thousand years or more, but they wouldn't survive Greenfield's saws. The trees were immensely strong and resilient but also fragile.

Like all life.

The light intensified before me. The trees were farther apart here. I could hear flowing water up ahead, and all at once I was leaving the forest and stepping to the edge of a cliff. I stopped three feet from the precipice, shed my pack, sat down, and scooted to the brink.

I was looking at a meadow. Verdant. Lush. Interlaced with crystalline streams and waterfalls.

Warm, slanting light bathed the clearing in a golden aura. Butterflies floated on the breeze. It was a landscape almost too sublime to take in, but instead of reveling in the beauty, I shivered, full of dread.

I'd seen the meadow before, fleetingly in my mind's eye, when Katherine, in her final moments, had told me of Greenfield's intentions.

They think that if they kill her, everything will be easier.

I knew now that I had come to the end of the path. My path, anyway.

I breathed. Tried to relax. Tried to comprehend what I was looking at and why it made me tremble so.

****

There was a small lake at the far end of the meadow. Round, flat calm, shimmering like platinum. Below me, perhaps seventy-five feet down, a rock as big as a mansion dominated the grassy plain like an island in a green sea. The massive stone lay broken—two jagged halves fallen slightly apart—as if smashed by the hammer of some outraged giant. There was a narrow pathway between the two halves, a winding, claustrophobic way largely hidden in shadow, but my eye was drawn to that trail, pulled inexorably to it like iron to a magnet.

Nothing moved on the section I could see, but I sensed that there was something farther back, deep within the stone, shielded by overhanging rock, concealed in darkness. I sensed that it—whatever it was—was coming closer, coming to find *me* specifically, and I couldn't turn away.

****

The golden halo enveloping the meadow

intensified. And several things happened at once.

A form moved on the trail bisecting the stone. It came forward, out of the darkness, out of the heart of the rock, stepping slowly.

It was a woman—an old woman, I guessed, from the way she walked—cloaked in a garment the color of the granite surrounding her. A hood concealed her face. She moved clear of the rock and stopped at the edge of the meadow.

There was a sound then, an awful, discordant sound in that place, at that moment—the faraway thump, thump, thump of helicopters approaching. The company's helicopters, I knew, coming to begin the assault on the valley. The rumble grew steadily, becoming a hideous heartbeat that reverberated off the peaks and ridges all around.

The old woman heard, too; I could tell from the cant of her head.

Rage swelled inside me then. Rage for my brother and at the thought of machines penetrating the valley. Rage at Holloway's deception and at Greenfield, for using me to open the sacred way for them.

The old woman raised her gnarled hands and pulled back her hood. Dark skin. Gray hair. Weathered, careworn face.

Bent but not broken.

She had a proud face. Beautiful. Regal. Kind. Wise. Somehow ancient and young at the same time. She lifted her eyes, and I saw that she was like someone who'd been asleep, like someone who's just stepped into a familiar room after a long time away. She was taking it all in, getting a read on things. But she was still unaware of Heidi. Unaware of me. Unaware of the unraveling that had just occurred in her sacred valley.

And then, in an instant, her face clouded. She hadn't known about the burning cabin and the old man, but now she did. She hadn't been aware that the beasts roamed free, but now she was. She hadn't perceived Holloway's deception, but now she saw it clearly.

She looked around, unafraid, lifted her head, found me at the edge of the cliff. Our eyes met, and I gasped, understanding washing over me in an instant, flooding my mind.

I know you. Though I'd never seen her before, I'd known her my entire life.

You are ... I struggled for her name and found that I lacked the language. I knew it in my bones, but I couldn't say it. Other words surfaced instead:

Natura. Eorthe. Nokomis—the Grandmother. Gaia. Mother nature. None of them sufficient or complete.

She takes this form to walk with us. She came because I summoned her.

What had the old man told me?

You opened the way and called to her, though unknowingly. And she will come—because that is the way of things. And she will die. In that form, she will die easily.

Greenfield wanted her dead. Heidi was going to kill her. And I knew in an awful flash of illumination what it would mean.

Not just the death of the natural world, already suffering under a thousand wounds and assaults, but part of humanity, as well. Our bond with the earth, the wild spirit in each of us, the source of creativity and wonder, the pulse of the planet.

The wild pulse of the planet, extinguished.

If the wild heart of the world died, I understood part of humanity would perish, as well. Our species might survive, but grace would bleed from the world. The power that binds us to Earth, the soil, the rain and wind and sun. The indescribable joy brought on by a sunrise, a crashing wave, a beam of sunlight in an emerald forest.

Directly below me, metal glinted.

It was Heidi, concealed in a jumble of broken rock at the base of the cliff, rising up, lifting her rifle, aiming at the old woman.

I saw her adjust the gun minutely, watched her finger curl around the trigger, saw the old woman's face darken as if she knew what was going to happen and accepted it.

There was no time to pull my own weapon. No time to find a rock to hurl down. I wanted Heidi dead, no question about that, but there was no time. Unless …

I pushed off hard from the cliff and jumped, aiming for Heidi, sure that I would die.

I saw her look up as she fired, missing the target. I saw the old woman track my fall, heard the thunder of the helicopters.

I smashed into Heidi, feet first, and the world went dark.

****

I awoke at the top of the mysterious pass, a few feet from the still-smoldering ruins of the old man's cabin.

I was lying on my back in the grass. Staring at the sky. Breathing. I had jumped more than six stories and lived. Or had I? I felt strong. The same, only …

I got to my feet and looked around for the old man,

knowing as I did so that he was gone, never to return. I stepped to the edge of the pass, where the outermost wall of the cabin had stood, and looked north toward Ranger Peak.

There were glints of metal in Holloway's staging area, but it was different now. A drawing-down of men and machines. An exodus from the mountains. How I knew this from such a great distance, I could not have explained. But I knew it all the same.

I realized, as I stood there watching, that they could no longer see the valley, that it had become hidden again. And I realized that I had awoken here, at the pass, for a reason. I remembered what I had agreed to do.

I will rebuild the cabin. I will live here, watching, standing guard.

A lonely role, but one I welcomed.

The Realm

Wanderings

"Don't forget, it's your turn to lead today," his father said as they loaded backpacks, snowshoes, thermoses of coffee and hot chocolate, and other supplies into the Land Cruiser. "Make sure you've got your map and compass."

It was early morning, still dark outside and very cold. Snow swirled around the driveway lights just beyond the open garage door. Andrew couldn't believe the big day had finally arrived.

Your turn to lead today.

For Christmas, his parents had given him a compass and an illustrated book on map reading. With his dad's help, he'd learned to use the compass on the trails around his neighborhood. He'd also practiced on his own. A lot. And apparently, he'd passed some sort of test because today he was going to lead his first real hike—a *winter* hike, no less—in Yellowstone National Park. A big deal for an eleven-year-old boy.

They drove through Gardiner with the defroster and heat on high, the wipers shushing back and forth, enough to sweep the huge, steadily falling snowflakes off the windshield. The town center was still asleep, only a couple of cars on the road and only a couple of businesses—one coffee shop and one gas station— illuminated and open. In summer, Andrew knew, Gardiner would be jammed with tour busses and giant RVs, tourists from every corner of the planet crowding the sidewalks. Hotels, restaurants, campgrounds, laundromats, coffee shops, and rafting and flyfishing outfitters would be booked to capacity, buzzing with activity dusk to dawn. But the summer chaos was months away. For now, the town and its world-famous two-million-acre neighbor mostly slumbered. It was Andrew's favorite time of year.

They drove through town to West Park Street, took the hairpin turn east, and made for a massive stone archway looming up ahead in the darkness.

The top of the fifty-foot-tall *Roosevelt Arch*—with a cornerstone set by Teddy himself in 1903—bore an inscription that was invisible in the dark, though Andrew knew it by heart: *"For the Benefit and Enjoyment of the People."*

They paused at the drive-through ranger station, and Malcolm, Andrew's father, exchanged good mornings with a fellow ranger—an older woman with a kind face and gray hair pulled back in a ponytail. She wore a perfectly pressed olive-green Park Service uniform, a broad-brimmed ranger hat, and a name tag that identified her as Lauren Jane Wilson. She smiled warmly at Andrew.

"Good morning, young man," she said. "What's your name?"

The boy, bundled in an oversized goose-down jacket and wool hat, made eye contact with the ranger. "I'm Andrew, ma'am."

"And where are you taking your father on this fine day, Andrew?"

"We're going snowshoeing, ma'am. In the Lamar Valley."

"Well, that sounds wonderful."

Malcolm told the ranger that Andrew would be

leading the hike.

Andrew beamed, and Ranger Wilson looked impressed. "No way," she said. "Do you have a map?"

"Yes, ma'am."

"How about a compass?"

"Yes, ma'am. Got one for Christmas. A good one." Andrew dug the compass out of his jacket pocket and showed it to her.

Ranger Wilson smiled. "Fantastic. You guys have a great day—and stay safe out there."

"Thank you, ma'am. We will."

They proceeded south into the park then, toward Mammoth Hot Springs and the junction with the Grand Loop Road. The sky ahead was beginning to lighten just a bit, but the snow was falling harder than ever.

They didn't talk much during the hour-long drive to the Lamar Valley—just admired the snowy sunrise. The highway was empty, and the roadbed lay hidden under a fresh blanket of snow.

They parked just west of Soda Butte, in a wide pullout overlooking the river, and stood at the open doors of the Land Cruiser, assembling their gear, and donning extra layers against the cold. The valley was still and quiet—save for the murmur of the frigid, slow-moving Lamar River meandering through the flats below the pullout. Huge, bare-limbed cottonwood trees fringed the river in places, and clusters of bison stood scattered across the valley floor, defying the cold, patient and stoic, imperturbable as blocks of granite.

By the time Andrew and his father had strapped on their snowshoes, slung packs onto their backs and adjusted their hiking poles, the heavy January clouds had begun to give way to watery blue skies. The temperature was twenty-five degrees Fahrenheit.

They descended to the flats and stepped to the river's edge. The Lamar was wide in this part of the valley and braided into four broad, shallow, gravel-bottomed channels that were relatively easy to ford. Taking their time and probing ahead with their hiking poles, they crossed each one—crunching noisily over the icebound sections and wading through the shallow, open water—the points of their snowshoes grinding on the gravel. The water—shockingly clear—seemed to be flowing in slow motion, as if it was trying to freeze. Andrew scanned for fish but didn't see any. In no place was the water more than nine or ten inches deep, and his feet stayed cozy inside his thickly lined snow boots.

Emerging from the river, they climbed a small hill and looked around. Andrew removed the topographic map from his jacket pocket, unfolded it, and checked it against the landscape and their position relative to the road. The pullout was clearly visible on the map.

After a minute, he spotted a narrow, snow-covered channel a few hundred yards to the west that intersected the main river near a stand of cottonwoods. "Over there," he said, pointing. "That's our starting point. I think."

"Lead on," said his dad. "You're the boss today."

They walked to the spot—Andrew breaking trail, getting used to the feel of the snowshoes—and stopped again beside the channel. Andrew consulted his map once more and the compass as well, holding it flat in his hand as his father had shown him and rotating the degree dial until the orienting and magnetic arrows aligned. He already knew they were facing south but confirmed it anyway. It seemed like something a real guide would do.

"Chalcedony Creek," Andrew said confidently, lowering the map. "That's what this little channel is."

He'd found the creek on the map days earlier at home, when his father had asked him to pick a route.

Malcolm Liggett nodded. "Good job. Now that we're here in person, what do you think?"

Andrew gazed south, tracing the snowbound creek—a barely discernable indentation, a furrow, in an endless blanket of white—across the valley floor and up the far ridge, where it disappeared into a grove of trees. He hadn't visited the Lamar since the previous summer, and the valley looked utterly different. They could hear water trickling deep under the snow at their feet.

The boy nodded. "I still think this is a good starting point." He frowned and looked at his father. "What do you think?"

The older man smiled. "I like it a lot. Now what's the plan?"

Andrew glanced at the map again. "Okay. We follow the creek across the valley and up the ridge. That's the first part."

"Lead on, boss." And then they were underway again, leaving the highway and civilization behind and marching into a slumbering, snowbound, achingly beautiful wilderness.

Andrew cut trail and set the pace, finding a comfortable gait with the snowshoes and poles. He found the act of leading exhilarating.

They paused after a mile or so to adjust their gear and look at a small herd of bison loitering near the river. The Lamar, after a languid southward curve across the valley floor, now lay directly to the east.

Peering through binoculars, Andrew watched the shaggy beasts forage for grass beneath the snow, using their massive, frost-festooned heads like shovels to shunt the snow aside. One huge bison, perhaps the dominant male of the herd, raised its head and peered in Andrew's direction.

The boy focused the binoculars and studied the creature's eyes—huge brown orbs that glistened and shone in the morning light. There was a *knowing* in those old eyes, Andrew thought—though he couldn't have put the idea into words. An innate, instinctual understanding of place, of seasons and cycles. A ferine wisdom incomprehensible to humans. The bison did not look away, and after several moments, Andrew had the uncanny feeling that it was *seeing* him—not as just a faraway blur—but actually perceiving him. Acknowledging his presence.

It was an absurd idea, the boy knew. Nonetheless, the moment lifted his already good mood and made him positively giddy.

He lowered the binoculars slowly and scanned the snow-blanketed valley horizon to horizon, feeling as he did so an electric thrill—faint at first—emanating from the ground, as if the whole of the plain was shivering with pent-up energy.

It wasn't an unrealistic notion, Andrew thought, given what his father had told him on numerous occasions—that much of Yellowstone was a super volcano. That the Earth beneath the park was "alive," in a manner of speaking. Why wouldn't the land around him be thrumming?

Andrew, grinning, his small body quivering with excitement, turned to tell his father what he was experiencing, certain that the older man was feeling it, too.

He stopped when he saw his father's face. The man appeared oddly preoccupied. Perhaps even a little troubled. Not a common condition for Malcolm Liggett.

Andrew held the binoculars out to share them, but the older man—his eyes fixed on the southern horizon—waved them away, saying nothing.

After a long moment, Malcolm's gaze flicked to the boy. He looked as if he'd just woken from an unpleasant dream. "We should get going," he said, mustering a wan and unconvincing smile. His voice sounded flat. "Daylight's burning."

And so Andrew said nothing—to anyone, ever—of the thrum and thrill, the strange, raw, wild energy he experienced that morning. But he never forgot it.

They walked side by side for a while after that, Malcolm still clearly preoccupied with something, his gaze repeatedly finding the southern horizon. The morning light intensified, and the two companions dug sunglasses out of jacket pockets and put them on.

At last, Malcolm seemed to shrug off whatever was bothering him. He paused on the trail and smiled at his son again, looking relaxed and engaged once more. "You go in front," he told the boy.

Following frozen Chalcedony Creek as it bent to the west, they began the long ascent of Specimen Ridge, leaving the valley behind and climbing through broad, open terrain interspersed with snow-mantled groves of Engelmann spruce and lodgepole pine.

Andrew settled into a slower pace as the grade steepened. Climbing through deep, untracked snow was hard work, and he focused on short-term goals, like reaching the next stand of trees and then the next. Glancing back, after climbing steadily for fifteen minutes, the boy was amazed at how far they'd traveled. Already they had a commanding view of the valley and the mountains to the east. Andrew spotted the Land Cruiser—just a speck now on the far side of the river. No other vehicles were visible on the road.

Climbing on, with nothing but wilderness before him, the boy's excitement intensified. His father had praised his plan for the hike, and—so far—offered no critique of his leadership. He reveled in the confidence and trust his dad had placed in him.

Even then, of course, Andrew knew who was *actually* in charge of the hike. Malcolm Liggett was, after all, a park ranger, a naturalist, a skilled backpacker and wilderness explorer hiking in a place he patrolled all the time. And he was an adult. The boy knew these things, yet knowing them did nothing to detract from his pride or sense of accomplishment. The fact that his father was allowing him to cut trail, set pace, and determine course and direction meant the world to him, and he savored the moment.

The sun climbed and the temperature warmed. The uppermost layer of snow froze into a thin crust that crunched and fractured satisfyingly as they tromped forward.

After an hour of steady walking, they abandoned slumbering Chalcedony Creek as it arced to the west, in favor of—Andrew hoped—an easier approach to the top of the ridge.

Climbing through open snowfields now, their breath coming in frosty plumes that caught the light and shimmered in the air, they reached a broad, flat bench set into the side of the ridge. The snow was deeper here and progress slower.

Andrew pushed forward—feeling tired after the climb but refusing to show it—and after ten more minutes spotted what he'd been hoping to see—another barely discernable furrow in the snow, this one running east and west across the ridge, winding away in both directions as far as the eye could perceive. Farther west along the furrow, slightly off to one side, Andrew spotted a chunk of brown painted wood jutting from the snow and recognized it for what it was—the top of a park service signpost. Whatever information was contained on the sign was concealed under the snow.

They stopped next to the sign, and Andrew consulted his map. Malcolm stood patiently nearby, leaning on his hiking poles, watching his son, saying nothing.

"Specimen Ridge Trail," said the boy after a couple of minutes. "That's what we're standing on." He looked up at his father questioningly. "Right?"

Malcolm smiled. "Pretend I'm not here. What do you think?"

Andrew considered it. He looked at the buried sign again. "I could just dig that out a little and read it."

His father laughed. "You could. But pretend the sign's not there either. Where are we?"

Andrew frowned, laid his pack on the snow, knelt beside it, and opened the map to its full size. Removing his gloves, he withdrew the compass from his jacket again—it hung from a lanyard around his neck—and laid it on top of the map, taking his time to orient the device. The summit of treeless, snow-covered Amethyst Mountain was clearly visible to the west, and Andrew took a bearing, concentrating hard, scrunching up his face and glancing alternately at the map and distant summit.

He nodded at last. "Definitely the Specimen Ridge Trail."

"Well done," said his father. "Well done. Now where we headed, boss? Are we sticking to your plan?"

Andrew nodded. "Yeah," he said. "Amethyst Mountain. We'll have lunch there and then follow Amethyst Creek back down into the valley and out to the road."

Malcolm Liggett nodded. "I like it."

Andrew hesitated.

"What?"

Andrew looked at the wide valley spread out below them and at 9,600-foot Cache Mountain and hulking, 10,900-foot Abiathar Peak to the east. Both summits were fringed with icy fog. The bench offered good visibility to the north, east and west. Hundreds of bison roamed near the river, and elk, as well. Undoubtedly there were other creatures wandering the folds of the land below or the remaining expanse of Specimen Ridge above. If they lingered awhile and used the binoculars, they might see a coyote, he thought. Or even a wolf. Also, he was suddenly incredibly hungry.

"This is nice here, too," said the boy, trying to sound grown up. Trying to say it like he imagined a real hiking guide might. "Might be a good spot for hot chocolate."

Malcolm Liggett laughed gently and squatted beside his son. "That is a fantastic idea. Maybe some apples and cheese, too? And some of your mom's cookies?

"Yeah!"

They spread a small tarp on the snow and sat facing the valley, scanning with the binoculars, munching snacks and sipping hot chocolate. They sat with their legs outstretched before them, the tails of their snowshoes buried in the snow.

Andrew, when it was his turn with the binoculars, focused on the Lamar where it angled south near Soda Butte. He counted at least a dozen snowbound streams that—like Chalcedony Creek—intersected with the larger waterway here and there. Soon enough, he knew, all of the streams would transform into shining silver ribbons, rushing and roaring with spring melt. For now, they lay dormant.

Andrew sat, marveling at the beauty around him and at his own sense of elation. The curious shiver of energy he'd experienced earlier had not abated; in fact, it was getting stronger, stirring his heart with a delightful, Christmas-morning kind of anticipation.

As he watched, enjoying the moment, enjoying the closeness to his dad—the person he admired most in all the world—he had the feeling that the day, *this particular day*, was somehow different from any other he'd ever experienced.

He couldn't have put it into words, but it felt as if, prior to this moment, he'd been observing the world through some sort of filter. Now the filter was lifting, the landscape changing in front of his eyes, transmuting, breaking open, revealing new wonders in the play of light and shadow on the lower reaches of the ridge and in the wind whispering through the barren branches of the aspen trees, arrayed like sentinels upon the bench.

Andrew paused, mid-sip, trying to make sense of what was happening. The air, for one thing, was different. Clearer than before, if that was possible, so that each rock and tree and hillock shimmered with new texture and detail.

The rocks are alive, he thought, almost believing it was true.

Andrew sat staring, flummoxed, wondering if the old bison he'd seen on the valley floor would understand what was going on. He felt certain that it would.

The curious energy coursing through his limbs—the same energy animating the rocks and trees and river, he was sure of it—touched his heart like an achingly beautiful melody, making it impossible not to smile.

Again he wanted to communicate what he was experiencing to his father, and again decided against it. The look on the older man's face had darkened once more. It was not a look that invited conversation.

Malcolm Liggett got to his feet and studied the sky above Specimen Ridge. They still had another five or six hundred feet to climb on the approach to Amethyst Mountain before they'd get a view south.

There was an odd tension in the man's six-foot-four-inch frame, Andrew thought. A tightness in his jaw that the boy found disquieting.

His father was almost always the embodiment of cool and calm. Supreme confidence. When veteran Ranger Malcolm Liggett showed up at any kind of conflict or disturbance in the park (frequent during the crazy, crowded summer months) his mere presence on the scene, his imposing, muscular bulk and intimidating glare (not to mention the fact that he was Black—an anomaly among the ranks of park service employees and a shock to many visitors) would diffuse most situations without the need for dialogue. Andrew knew that his father took pride in his stature and abilities.

At the moment, though, he appeared oddly discomfited. Clearly something was still troubling him.

"What're you looking at, Dad?" the boy asked.

The older man shook his head. "Nothing much, really. The sky. There's a weird cast to it is all."

"You think it's gonna storm again or something?"

The older man laughed. "Or something," he said. "Forecast called for increased clearing, but…" his voice trailed off.

Andrew watched his father, waiting for him to continue.

Malcolm Liggett made a slow three-hundred-and-sixty-degree turn in the snow, taking in the entirety of the landscape. He sniffed the air. "Do you smell anything?"

Andrew sniffed the air, too. "Pine trees?"

The older man shook his head, perplexed. "No. It smells like…" He hesitated. "Like spring," he said. He looked baffled. "Or it *did*, a minute ago. I swear I got a whiff of something just now—like a meadow in bloom."

"Mom has lotion like that," said Andrew.

Malcolm Liggett laughed, and the tension disappeared from his face. He smiled at his son. "Maybe that's what I'm thinking of," he said. "Your mom's lotion. Or maybe your old man is just losing his marbles." He dropped back down next to his son and rolled his eyes like a crazy person. They both laughed.

"Okay," said Malcolm, after a minute. "We should get moving if we're gonna make it to the top of Amethyst and down before dark."

"Let's do it," said Andrew.

"Hang on," said Malcolm, withdrawing a little journal from the mesh pouch at the top of his backpack. "Forgot about this. Something I wanted to read out here. Something that relates to our hike."

The boy looked at him quizzically.

"Don't worry, it's quick."

Malcolm opened the journal and unfolded a sheet of paper tucked inside. He pulled a pair of reading glasses from his jacket pocket and put them on.

Andrew waited patiently. Reading was a ritual that happened on almost every hike or ski trip the two companions took together. At some point during the day, Malcolm Liggett would share a carefully selected passage from a book or article with his son. Sometimes the passage was historical. Sometimes it had to do with plants or animals or geology. Sometimes it was humorous. Andrew remembered hearing "Green Eggs and Ham" on one early childhood camping trip. Occasionally, it was a poem or short story.

The ritual was one that Andrew loved, in part because it made the whole day more special. Clearly his father put effort into selecting the passages he chose to share. It made the boy feel valued. Loved. Which he was.

Malcolm Liggett looked at his son. "I've told you about John Muir," he said. "Do you remember?"

Andrew nodded. "The old guy with the beard who hiked in the mountains for days with just an apple in his pocket. Did he *really* do that?"

Malcolm Liggett laughed. "He may have had more than one apple, probably some bread, too, but yeah, that's the guy."

"You showed me some pictures," said Andrew, "in one of our Yellowstone books."

"Right. So what was his favorite thing in the world, do you think?"

Andrew thought about it. "Hiking?"

"Exactly. John Muir loved to hike. But here's the thing—he did not like the word itself."

Andrew scratched his wool hat. "Didn't like the word 'hiking'? That's weird."

Malcolm lifted the paper he was holding and adjusted his glasses. "Check it out." He read:

"'I don't like either the word or the thing,' Muir said. 'People ought to saunter in the mountains—not hike! Do you know the origin of that word 'saunter?' It's a beautiful word. Away back in the Middle Ages people used to go on pilgrimages to the Holy Land, and when people in the villages through which they passed asked where they were going, they would reply, 'A la sainte terre,' 'To the Holy Land.' And so they became known as sainte-terre-ers or saunterers. Now these mountains are our Holy Land, and we ought to saunter through them reverently, not 'hike' through them."

Malcolm lowered the paper and looked at his son. "What do you think of that?"

Andrew frowned. Thought about it. "I still like the word 'hike.'"

Malcolm laughed. "Me, too. But do you get what he's saying?"

Andrew appraised his surroundings and nodded. "The mountains are holy. Like church?"

"I think that's right," said Malcolm. "*I* think they are."

"I do, too," said the boy. Andrew thought about what he'd been feeling all morning—the curious thrum of energy. The sense that the trees and rocks were alive.

Especially today it feels holy, he wanted to say. *Especially with the light the way it is and everything buzzing and humming.* But he kept this to himself.

Donning their packs once more, they trekked on, following the faint imprint of the Specimen Ridge Trail up the eastern flank of Amethyst Mountain.

The sun arced higher, and the last remnants of fog disappeared from the folds and hollows of the ridge. The views of the valley and surrounding lands grew ever more dramatic as they climbed, until it seemed that they could see the entire northern quarter of the two-million-acre park. The sky—a deep, royal blue now—encapsulated the terrain, holding it, containing it, like the dome of a snow globe. The air was crisp and clean and shockingly, preternaturally clear.

Only the land to the south remained unseen, unknowable, shielded from view by the remaining bulk of the ridge. At the summit of Amethyst Mountain, or slightly before, the travelers knew the views would open all around, giving them a bird's-eye look at Yellowstone in every direction, in all its winter glory. It was the reason Andrew had chosen the summit as their destination.

Climbing through pristine, untracked fields of white, drawing closer to the top with every thoughtful step and pole plant, the Liggetts imagined and anticipated the goal ahead in vastly different ways.

For the boy, the summit held the key—he hoped—

to a magical, wonderful mystery he could not wait to solve. The strange buzz of excitement that had been building inside of him all morning—the sense that he was somehow close to understanding a fantastic secret—intensified as he walked, inducing a Zen-like feeling of peace and oneness with his surroundings.

Walking steadily, rhythmically, the boy focused on the untouched snow directly ahead, on a phenomenon he'd never witnessed before. The sun, refracting off the pristine field of white, had turned the uppermost layer of ice crystals into tiny prisms—billions of minute lenses dispersing the colors of the rainbow. The effect was subtle but clearly visible if you were paying attention.

The boy, in his meditative state, marching forward, utterly oblivious to fatigue, thirst, or hunger, zeroed in on the colors, imagining after a while that he was seeing the crystals on a microscopic level—as if he'd shrunk to 1/1,000 of his normal size. In his mind's eye, crystals towered all around him like cathedral windows, bathing him in ethereal, multi-hued light.

He thought about the passage his father had read— about the mountains being "holy." Smiling, his heart swelling with contentment, he knew in his bones that it was true.

****

For Malcolm Liggett, the walk to the top of Amethyst Mountain—something he'd done at least a dozen times before—brought with it a bewildering, growing sense of dread.

The feeling had been with him all day, starting on the drive to the trailhead—a small amorphous anxiety in the back of his mind. And though he'd tried mightily, he could not quell the belief that something was amiss. Or soon would be.

It made no sense. The weather was fine. He felt rested and strong. Their gear—with one irritating exception—was in good order, and the trek Andrew had proposed was easily within the boy's capabilities.

I should be smiling. Happy.

He'd been looking forward to the outing as much as his young son, after all, envisioning it as an opportunity to share a beloved place and teach Andrew some valuable wilderness skills at the same time.

He'd tried to analyze the feelings of disquiet, telling himself over and over that there was no cause for concern.

True, there *was* an "odd cast to the sky," as he'd said to Andrew. Something different about the light—a weird shimmer above the southern horizon that Malcolm had never seen before and couldn't explain. The light did not portend bad weather as far as he could tell, but it left him feeling unsettled all the same.

There were other oddities, too. Seemingly trivial anomalies in the fabric and flow of the day. Barely noticeable irregularities that triggered faint alarms in the recesses of his brain.

The utter emptiness of the highway after the turn at Tower Junction, for example. *Not a single car on the Northeast Entrance Road?* Strange. There were always a few cars—Park Service vehicles at the very least—transiting the link between Cooke City and the outside world. Even in deepest winter.

The paucity of cars made Malcolm suspect a traffic accident or worse. Perhaps a bridge or roadbed failure somewhere behind them. He wondered if maybe a plow had gone off the road.

He checked his Park Service-issue two-way radio as they were dropping into the valley, half expecting to be asked to assist with an emergency on his day off (Andrew would understand, he thought) and discovered that the device was unusable. It powered up fine, same as the 50,000 other odd times he'd used it in the course of work and leisure. This morning, though, there was only static on the dial. Static on every channel. Nothing remotely approaching a normal signal. The battery was working—clearly—but something else was screwed up.

After they parked, he tried tightening the antenna. He unscrewed the back cover and checked for loose wires. There were no problems that he could see. Then again, he wasn't a technician. The park had a couple of radio experts on staff, but he wasn't one of them. He left the useless device in the car, saying nothing of the matter to Andrew.

The very act of leaving the radio behind induced a twinge of anxiety in Malcolm Liggett. He liked carrying a radio. Even on a simple day hike. The radio was standard backcountry ranger gear—along with a first aid kit, emergency shelter, and Smith & Wesson Model 29 revolver (which he still had on his belt and presumably still worked). The fact that his typically dependable two-way—something he'd relied on for the better part of a decade—had chosen this particular morning to conk out was annoying and vaguely troubling. He wondered—uncharacteristically—if it was a harbinger of things to come.

Gripping his hiking poles and following his son down from the pullout and across the river, Malcolm Liggett sought to reason his concerns away.

So what if the radio's busted? It's a perfect day, and we're taking a kid's hike, for God's sake. I could do this blindfolded. Backwards. And who cares if the road is quiet? Quiet is good. Quiet is great. How often does anyone get the Lamar to themselves? What the hell's wrong with me?

Malcolm Liggett *did* like quiet. And solitude. They were two of the things he loved most about wilderness. Except, if he was being honest with himself, the "solitude" of this particular morning felt somehow different. He couldn't put his finger on it, but it did. *Different.*

Surveying the countryside, taking in the whole of the Lamar Valley, the river, the ridges, the mountains all around (a landscape he knew as well as his own backyard) Malcolm Liggett had the bizarre sense that the land was waiting for something. Holding its breath. That the world—at least the part he could see—was on the verge of some momentous event. It occurred to him—out of the blue—that a kind of cosmic countdown had begun, that all of creation was watching to see what would happen next.

There's an earthquake coming. That's it. He knew animals could sense such things. Maybe what he was feeling was some kind of biologically based premonition.

Or maybe I'm sick. Maybe I have a virus. A brain tumor.

Such anxiety, such self-analysis, was completely out of character for Malcolm Liggett. He hadn't stressed over anything this much in decades. Not since working himself into a tizzy trying to ask his future wife on a date. Beloved by friends and colleagues for his calm, comforting, rational demeanor, he was the antithesis of a fretful person.

So what the hell is going on? Here I am climbing through untracked snow on a bluebird day with my amazing kid leading the way, and I'm spinning over the stupidest shit.

It made no sense, and he tried again to sweep it all away, resolving to make an appointment with his doctor in Livingston as soon as he got home. It'd been a couple of years since his last checkup, come to think of it.

****

The two companions walked in silence. The open summit of Amethyst Mountain lay just a few hundred yards ahead now, a dazzling white dome against a clean blue sky. Andrew was glad he had his sunglasses on. Even with the shades, he found himself squinting.

He pulled his compass from his pocket, just for the heck of it, and eyed the device curiously. The needle was spinning crazily, dancing this way and that, as if someone was holding a magnet over the needle. Andrew thought about stopping to fiddle with it and rejected the idea. They were almost to the top. He could troubleshoot the compass later.

In another few minutes, the boy realized, they'd crest the ridge and finally get a clear look to the south. The idea thrilled him, though he did not know why.

The answers are there. He could not have explained why he thought this or where the notion had come from.

Climbing, listening to his own breathing, to the steady, reassuring thud of his heart, Andrew heard—or felt—another sound intertwining with his own internal rhythms. Soft and delicate and almost imperceptible at first, it flowed like music.

The strange composition—alternately bright and uplifting, mournful and melancholy—was unlike anything he'd ever heard before. Intermingling with his thoughts before he was even aware of it, the music flowed between his breaths and soared with his heartbeat as he pushed for the summit. Like the exhilarating thrum of energy he'd experienced after crossing the river, the music—sublime, ethereal, and profoundly moving—seemed to emanate from the ground itself.

Andrew stopped climbing. Malcolm stopped a few paces behind, saying nothing. The boy listened, expecting to hear the strange music more clearly. Instead, it dissolved, vanishing from his consciousness like vapor.

He listened harder, willing the music to resume, experiencing an almost physical pain as the sound faded. He could hear the rustle of his father's jacket now and the lonely sighing of the breeze around the peak. Nothing more.

It was just in my head. Andrew wondered how he could have conjured such a dreamy, exquisite melody and why it stopped when he stopped moving. He wished his piano teacher in Gardiner could have heard it.

"What's up?" asked his father.

"Thought I heard something."

"Like what?"

"Music. Thought I heard music. Dumb, huh? Way out here."

Malcolm removed his sunglasses and studied his

son. Then the valley spread wide below them. There was a pained expression on his face.

"What?" said Andrew.

The older man smiled. "Not dumb," he said. "The mountains have their own music. I hear it myself sometimes. Let's keep going. We're almost there."

****

Walking the final few paces to the summit that day, witnessing the rapturous blue of the sky and the radiance of the noonday sun, any hiker would have anticipated glorious views in all directions.

That's not what Andrew and Malcolm found.

Ascending, finally, to the snowy cap of the peak, the walkers discovered, to their amazement, the land to the south—all of it—concealed beneath a sea of fat, rapidly moving clouds.

Along with the wholly unexpected view came a rush of sudden, unanticipated noise, as if they'd just cleared some kind of soundproof barrier.

The companions stood staring, dumbstruck, saying nothing, trying to process the scene before them.

They were above the clouds—barely. The nearest ones looked almost close enough to touch. Ever-changing fissures in the ocean of gray revealed, fleetingly, a verdant land in the thrall of an ebullient spring rainstorm. Thunder boomed below them, echoing off distant peaks and valleys. They'd heard no rumor of thunder whatsoever during their climb. Now it was a symphony at full volume, a cacophony of bone-shaking crashes and rumbles.

The heady scent of rain-washed pine forests and flower-filled alpine meadows enveloped the travelers, yanking them from deep winter to full spring in one utterly jarring and disorienting moment.

The thunder subsided momentarily, and they heard the roar of waterfalls on the cloud-veiled slopes below.

The curious excitement and anticipation that Andrew had been feeling all day reached its zenith on the mountaintop, and he trembled with joy. Sheer elation. Far from being intimidated by the surreal sights and sounds, he wanted nothing more than to run full speed downhill into the strange, foreign land. Because truth be told, at that moment, it did not feel strange or foreign at all. It felt familiar. Welcoming. As if he'd seen it before. As if it'd been beckoning to him for years. Since earliest childhood.

Andrew turned from the Eden below and looked at his father, who clearly was not having the same kind of experience. The man appeared terrified. Eyes wide. Jaw slack. He whipped around—pivoting 180 degrees in a series of jerking half steps, tossing powder into the air with his snowshoes—and stared in the opposite direction. Andrew did the same. The view this way had not changed.

There was the Lamar Valley, right where they'd left it, white and pristine beneath a cold winter sun. There was frigid Cache Mountain and ice-bedecked Abiathar Peak. The view this way presented the expected—a frosty, somnolent world months from waking.

The companions looked south again as another rush of warm, scented air washed over the peak, and it seemed to Andrew that they were teetering between two seasons, two worlds, two realities.

There has to be a reason for this. And the answer is down there. In the meadows. In the forests.

He looked at his father again. The man was trying to speak, working his jaw. But no sound was coming out. He looked so panicked that Andrew wondered if he might be having a heart attack. The boy's grandfather had died of a heart attack the previous year. He knew what a heart attack was.

The cloud deck opened wide below them, splitting abruptly in two and pulling apart, reminding Andrew of a Sunday School story he'd heard about Moses opening a passageway through the Red Sea. He'd never believed the bible story—not for a moment—but he believed the scene unfolding below them.

The tear in the clouds revealed a lush, verdant land of flower-filled meadows and vast forests of immense, towering trees. Shafts of warm spring sunlight shone down through cracks in the grey ceiling, illuminating colossal waterfalls and a broad, wild valley.

The hurrying clouds separated even farther, opening a view of the southern horizon and a line of snow-covered peaks taller than any Andrew had ever seen.

"The Absarokas," said the boy, doubting the statement as soon as it was out of his mouth.

Malcolm Liggett found his voice at last, low and strangled. "Those aren't the Absarokas. Those aren't...real."

Malcolm took a single tottering step downhill, toward the strange land, toward the place—just yards away—where the deep snow gave way, impossibly, to green grass and flowers. He moved haltingly, hesitantly, as if he didn't want to go, didn't want to see, yet couldn't stop himself—like a man approaching a gruesome accident.

"Dad, wait!" Andrew cried, his voice subsumed by a fresh peal of thunder. The clouds slammed together again, blocking the view of the faraway peaks and curling upward to caress the top of Amethyst Mountain. Tentacles of fog swirled around the boy. "Dad," he called again. "What are you doing?"

Malcolm Liggett lurched downhill—away from his son, away from winter, away from the world he'd always known—like a drunk. Someone in a trance. He seemed not to have heard Andrew's question.

It came to the boy in an instant what he needed to do.

Though he wanted more than anything to follow his father—no, to lead the way—he understood on an almost instinctual level that doing so would end in disaster for one or both of them.

I know this place, but my father does not. I can venture here, but he cannot—not without suffering. Not without pain.

If I lead, or follow him into this land, we will not find our way back. We will not see Mom again. We will not see our house again. I will not see Indigo or Tiger or Grandpa Miles again.

How he knew this he could not say, but he knew it in his bones, in his cells.

"Dad!" he screamed.

The older man kept going.

"Dad! Help."

Malcolm flinched as if he'd been struck. He halted. Looked up at the boy distractedly. Annoyed. "What's wrong?"

"We need to go," said Andrew, pointing toward the Lamar. "This way."

The fog was all around them now, washing over the summit like a silent sea, blocking the sun and plunging the world into a twilight gloom. Andrew tore his sunglasses from his eyes.

"This way, Dad. Come back. Please."

The older man waved the boy away dismissively and turned again. Took another step. Then another. He reached the edge of the snow, bent down, and plucked a red flower from the meadow. Standing once more, he twirled the flower in his fingers, staring at it like someone in a trance.

Thunder rumbled anew, crashing and cracking. The noise was close, violent, like vast slabs of granite smashing together. The sound ricocheted off distant cliffs and canyons like cannon fire.

Andrew lunged forward, forgetting the snowshoes strapped to his boots, and almost fell on his face. "Dad!" he screamed again. "Mom is waiting for us. We have to go. Right now. Or we won't see her again!"

Malcolm swung around once more, a flicker of comprehension in his eyes this time. His trance-like expression morphing into a look of pure bewilderment. He studied his son and seemed to notice the fog for the first time.

"We need to go, Dad," Andrew repeated, extending his gloved hand. "This way."

The older man nodded and, keeping his back to the strange land, began to ascend once more. It was snowing now, steadily, dimming the light even more.

Malcolm pulled even with the boy and paused, breathing hard. Harder than he needed to be. Hyperventilating, practically.

It dawned on Andrew that his father was trying to

control his fear. Keep panic at bay. The flower he'd been holding slipped from his fingers and lay on the snow, the vivid red of the petals like a splash of blood against the white.

"Your hike, kiddo," Malcolm Liggett whispered, forcing a smile. "Get us outta here."

Andrew bent, plucked the flower from the ground, wrapped it carefully in a Kleenex, and placed the little package gently, delicately, in his inside breast pocket. His father, staring catatonically into space, did not see him do this.

"This way, Dad. Follow me." The boy tugged his hip belt tight and leapt downhill, making for the road, the Land Cruiser, safety, following the same trail they'd used on the way in. He'd intended to make a loop northward, down Amethyst Creek and back to the road that way, but given the clouds, the snow, and what had just happened, that plan struck him as foolhardy. Far easier, he thought, to just follow their own footprints home.

Dense fog flowed around them, transforming noon into night and making it hard to see more than a few paces ahead. Andrew dug a headlamp from a pouch on the side of his pack without pausing and flipped it on with a swipe of his gloved hand. The light cut a crisp swath through the mist, illuminating a tunnel of huge, fat flakes, but it did little to improve visibility. The boy snapped the light off, shoved it into a pocket, and plowed forward, confident of the direction regardless of the light. "It's this way, Dad," he called. "Stay with me."

After less than a minute of fast walking, the sounds behind them faded. The thunder died away. The noise of water—of spring rain and crashing waterfalls—receded to a whisper, and then nothing, as if devoured by the mist.

Andrew sniffed the air. It smelled like winter again. Like snow. Like Yellowstone in January. No scent of flowers or rain or forests at the height of spring. And though the boy did not hear a door closing, he sensed, as he careened downhill—using gravity and momentum to hurl himself over and through the drifts—that one had slammed behind them.

The snow was falling so heavily now that it was difficult to see their old tracks.

The sky was perfectly clear a few minutes ago, Andrew observed detachedly. *Now it's blizzarding.*

It was an impossibly fast change, even for Yellowstone. He thought about asking his father to explain the abrupt shift in the weather—it was practically a whiteout now—but sensed without looking that the man was just as confused as he was, or more so, and still recovering from the events at the top.

Descending, following the rapidly vanishing trail, Andrew tried to analyze what had happened on the summit—and found it oddly, painfully difficult to do so.

Memories just minutes old now were muddled and remote, jumbled, and fragmented, as if they were being blown up and wiped from his mind, obliterated as quickly as the footprints they were following. The things he'd witnessed on the peak floated in the periphery of his consciousness, like shards of dreams, ephemeral and fleeting.

Only they weren't dreams. The things we saw were real. This isn't right. I should stop and ask Dad what's going on.

He thought better of the idea. *He doesn't know any more than I do. Stopping now will be a waste of time. And maybe dangerous—the storm the way it is.*

Instead, he ignored the cold and the fatigue settling into his bones and led the way downhill, while at the same time straining—hard enough to give himself a headache—to recall what had transpired on the summit and cement some of it in his mind.

Because he did *so* want to remember what he'd witnessed—the forests, the thunder, the rain-washed meadows. Most of all, he wanted to remember the far mountains—mountains that appeared to touch the lower reaches of space. He fought and struggled and repeated to himself as he walked the story of the wonders he'd seen.

Locked in struggle—against the storm and the inexorable theft of his memories—the boy had an epiphany.

The land is taking my memories. Defending itself. Concealing itself. Maybe we weren't supposed to see what we saw. Maybe no one's supposed to. He wrestled with the notion. *But then why did I feel so welcome there? Why was I drawn to the peak? Why have I been anticipating it all day, all week, all month, since I first found this place on the map?*

He thought and wondered and contemplated, but it was a mystery he could not solve.

****

The fog lifted as they neared the base of Specimen Ridge, and the snowfall lessened, then ceased altogether. Andrew could see the river in the distance now and the faint outline of the road. But it was getting dark—fast.

How can it be getting dark already? We were on top at noon. The walk down couldn't have taken more than an hour and a half.

It made no sense. But the day's timeline—when he thought about it—seemed as amorphous and difficult to reconcile as the things they'd seen.

Andrew realized all at once that his father was walking alongside him, matching his pace, and could tell simply by the man's gait and presence that he was feeling better.

"Well done," said the older man. "Not much farther now. But my gosh, it's later than I realized. I'm starving—bet you are, too."

"Yeah," said Andrew. "We didn't eat our lunches."

Malcolm stopped in his tracks and looked at his son. Concerned. Confused. "We didn't?"

Andrew shook his head. "Huh-uh. They're still in our packs."

Malcolm traced the route they'd just descended with his eyes. Four or five hundred yards above them, the trail vanished into fog. The summit was completely hidden. Malcolm stood, peering into the gray, the growing darkness, and it struck Andrew that his father was trying to recall what had happened. Evidently his memories were fading, too.

He doesn't remember. Doesn't remember the thunder or the waterfalls or the meadows or the mountains. His memories are even more messed up than mine.

The realization, simultaneously reassuring and terrifying, crystallized in the boy's mind, and he knew what he needed to do.

Watching his father, he had the sense that if the man stared long enough, hard enough, he *would* recall something. Not specifics, probably, but feelings—of fear, doubt, and uncertainty that would dwell in his mind and eat at him. How the boy knew this, he could not say, but his course of action was clear. He wanted to spare the man the anguish he'd seen in his face earlier in the day.

"It was the snow," said the boy. "It started dumping, remember? We had to get outta there."

Malcolm regarded him skeptically. "The snow," he said, repeating it softly. "The snow." Andrew could tell he was trying process the idea.

"Yeah," Malcolm said at last. "I guess that's it. Didn't eat our lunches 'cause of the snow. Of course, you're right."

They resumed walking, in silence, and reached the valley floor. They saw headlights on the distant road and heard the grinding, scraping noise of a plow.

"We're gonna be home late," said Malcolm. "Hopefully, Mom hasn't called out the troops."

"Just get her on the radio," said Andrew.

"Left the radio in the car," said Malcolm. "Thing's busted. There's a payphone at Tower Junction. I'll call her from there."

But when they reached the Land Cruiser and Malcolm tried the radio again—for the heck of it—he found, to his great surprise, that it worked perfectly.

"Very odd," he told his son. "Thing was useless as a brick when we left here. I'm taking it to the shop at Old Faithful on Monday. Can't have it acting up like this when I'm working."

Malcolm radioed his wife to tell her they were safe.

She sounded relieved and said she had not "called out the troops" but had been on the verge of doing so. She told Malcolm she'd made a nice dinner and couldn't wait to see "her boys."

They drove home in darkness, wolfing the sandwiches and other snacks they'd intended to eat on the summit.

Malcolm took his time on the freshly plowed road, alert to the possibility of black ice. He found an AM station playing old Johnny Cash hits and set the volume on low.

Andrew peered into the darkness through the Land Cruiser's windows, fighting sleep, struggling—still—to remember the day's surreal revelations.

The vehicle was warm, Johnny Cash's voice low and soothing, and the boy wearier than he'd ever been in his life. Drowsiness overtook him before Tower Junction, and he slept all the way to Mammoth Hot Springs, slumped against the passenger door.

Waking in the comforting darkness of the Land Cruiser, now just minutes from home, the boy looked at his father.

Malcolm Liggett's gaze was fixed on the road, his face illuminated by the glow of the instrument panel. There were circles around his eyes and a weary sag to his shoulders. When he saw that his son was awake, he straightened and smiled and ruffled the boy's hair.

"What a day," said Malcolm. "I'm starving—even after that sandwich."

"Me, too."

The car went quiet for another mile, Andrew struggling with a question he was afraid to ask.

"What'd you think of the view, Dad?" he said at

last. "From the top of Amethyst Mountain, I mean?"

Malcolm glanced at him and then his glaze flicked back to the road. For a moment, Andrew thought he looked doubtful, confused, as if he'd just recalled a troubling thought. The look passed and he shrugged. "Well, man," he said. "I mean, we couldn't see too much with that crazy storm, could we?" He smiled and ruffled the boy's hair again. "Don't worry, though— we'll go back up when it's clear so you can see all around. The Absarokas are a sight to behold, lemme tell ya."

He doesn't remember. The land took his memories, and he doesn't recall what happened. But I do. I do, a little bit, at least. Though in the weeks, months, and years that followed, the memories he'd struggled so hard to save and cement during the descent from Amethyst Mountain became more and more fragmented, like half-remembered scenes from old movies or snippets of long-ago dreams.

That night after dinner, ready to collapse from fatigue, Andrew climbed the stairs to his bedroom and hung his jacket from a hook on the back of the door.

He stopped, a familiar scent catching his attention and making his heart jump. He unzipped the jacket's inside breast pocket and slowly, painstakingly, removed the tissue-wrapped package. He'd forgotten all about it. Even as he lifted it—amazed by its near weightlessness—he could not recall what was inside. Only that it was something special. Something he did not want to damage.

Setting the tiny packet on his desk, heart thumping, he carefully peeled back the layers of tissue until the flower, now flattened and curled in on itself, fetus-like, lay completely revealed. The boy whistled softly and fell into his chair, feeling suddenly dizzy. Lightheaded. The room and all of his belongings receded around him, then disappeared completely as the strange flower filled his vision and held him motionless.

Memories of the day's surreal events washed over him in a jumbled, confusing wave, overwhelming his tired brain, frightening him and at the same instant igniting his imagination and curiosity. He remembered the vividness of the red petals against the snow and saw now that the flower's radiance had not diminished.

And yet, even as he watched, it drained of color and faded. The fading caused him to feel helpless and triggered a bone-deep ache that made him want to cry out in pain. He quickly covered the flower, waited awhile, then pulled the tissue back once more. Too late. The luminous quality he'd witnessed so fleetingly was gone.

This can't be happening. Things don't just fade like this. It's the light in my room. Or I'm not looking at it right. I'm so tired.

But he knew the truth. When he'd first unwrapped it, moments earlier, the flower had fairly blazed— shimmering and flaring like a magical trinket. Alive, it had seemed, a rare and wild thing trapped and caged. It was completely out of place in his room, making all of his other things appear shabby by comparison. Dull and colorless.

Now, as if somehow sensing its new surroundings, the flower's essence was bleeding away, and it was blending with its surroundings. Not disappearing exactly but becoming ordinary. *Acceptable to human eyes.*

He remembered a wolf he and his father had seen the previous summer during a day hike near Slough Creek inside the park. The creature—a juvenile male recently exiled from his pack, according to Malcolm—had emerged from an alder thicket a hundred yards away, its magnificent amber coat backlit by the setting sun. The encounter had lasted no more than ten seconds before the wolf vanished over a rise, but it left a powerful impression. The boy had been struck by the creature's grace and strength, the silent, effortless way it moved, and most of all by its wildness—by the *otherness* reflected in its eyes, as if it possessed power and knowledge he would never understand. He had *so* wanted to understand. Wanted to travel where the wolf traveled, know what it knew. He daydreamed after the encounter about capturing such an animal and holding it.

Then I'd know its secrets.

He'd told his father of his daydream and his wish to own a wolf or a wolf hybrid (he'd seen some around Gardiner), and instead of passing judgment or criticizing the idea, his father had taken him on a field trip to a tourist attraction near Livingston, a gaudy, highway-side mini-zoo called "Montana Safari" housing wolves and bears that had, one way or another, crossed paths with humans or livestock and couldn't be reintroduced into the wild.

The boy had comprehended the silliness—the *wrongness*—of his daydream immediately upon entering the attraction. The wolves and bears who lived there, though still beautiful, were pitiful shadows of their wild brethren. The noisy, popcorn-eating tourists gawking at the beasts didn't seem to notice or care. But the scene pained young Andrew Liggett. He'd seen wild wolves and bears—watched for hours through binoculars and spotting scopes as they frolicked and foraged on sun-dappled meadows, and these animals seemed almost dead by comparison. The fierce light he'd seen in the wild wolf's gaze did not exist here. It was nowhere to be found. These animal's eyes were vacant. Dull.

Without his father saying a word, it struck the boy that the very act of capturing, holding, and containing the creatures had obliterated their spirits. They moved like cattle, listless and bored. Disconnected from their motherland like a limb cut from a body. The creatures in the compound might dream of open space or feel the primordial tug of the moon deep in their veins, but the bond with their ancestral home was sundered. They would die caged and contained, broken and subdued, not under the light of stars but the stark glow of the compound's fluorescents.

"What did you think?" his father asked as they were leaving the exhibit.

Andrew considered it. "I'm glad they're alive," he said. "It's neat they could be rescued. But they don't seem too happy. I think they miss their real home."

The animals Andrew had seen in the compound had lost their wildness, and it was somehow the same with the flower, though the boy doubted whether something so small even had a "spirit," as he understood the word. Regardless, its life force was fading. Draining away.

He pondered what to do with the flower. It seemed wrong to keep it. And just as wrong to throw it away. He thought about burying it or returning it to the mountaintop and wondered when he might have such an opportunity. In the end, he placed the flower carefully inside a book—a thick, forty-year-old geology textbook his grandfather had given him, returned the book to his bookcase, and went to bed, resolving to consider the issue anew in the morning.

Just before he fell asleep, the boy, age eleven, said a prayer as he always did. It was his personal version of a famous children's prayer and the one he'd used for years. How or when he'd adapted it, he could not recall. He'd been very small at the time. Probably his mother had helped him. Night after night, he said the words in the same cadence, in the same whisper, reciting the familiar, comforting lines without really thinking about them. The prayer was part of his routine, like brushing his teeth.

"Now I lay me down to sleep," he whispered, already drifting off, his limbs heavy and motionless, his head cradled in his soft pillow. "I pray the Lord my soul to keep. If I shall die before I wake, I pray the Lord my soul to take, and this I ask for Jesus's sake. God bless Mom and Dad and Grandpa Miles and Indigo and Tiger. God bless the good people and let them stay good, and bless the bad people and let them become good and kind. Bless the slaves and let them be free. Bless the poor people and let them have more food and money. Bless the animals and birds and the forests and the mountains we found in the snow, and help my Daddy not be afraid."

His eyes flew open in the dark, and he sat bolt upright.

"We saw those mountains *today*," he whispered to no one, recalling the peaks with sudden, startling clarity. *That was today. Dad was afraid today.*

And yet, the mountains (*the very same mountains*), were already in his prayer.

He sat there, frightened and confused. He'd been saying the prayer exactly this way for as long as he could remember, without even registering the words, without noticing them.

Have I seen those mountains before today? he wondered. *On an earlier hike?* He knew, even as he posed the question to himself, that he had. The feeling of déja vu was overwhelming. But *where* had he seen them? *When*? On these points, his memory was as opaque and unyielding as the darkness surrounding him. He could recall nothing specific whatsoever.

He sighed and fell back on his mattress in exhaustion. Nothing about the strange mountains seemed solid or permanent or verifiable. It was all so confusing. He lay there—fatigue overtaking him at last—and slept peacefully for eleven hours. By morning, all memory of the flower and the place he'd hidden it had vanished from his mind. And when he said his prayer that night, the phrases flowed easily as always, and he hesitated only for an instant when he came to the part about the mountains in the snow.

****

Memories of the far mountains returned to Andrew Liggett in his dreams and in rare, waking moments throughout his school years and during his military training and deployment. The memories were invariably potent but fleeting. Transitory.

Sometimes it was a splash of red that triggered a memory. A red closely matching the color of the flower he'd seen on Amethyst Mountain. Sometimes it was a thunderclap, close and deafening. Most often what conjured the memories was sunlight. Sunlight filtered in a particular way—through rain-scrubbed air across a sea of hurrying clouds. The right sort of light made him stop and picture in his mind spires of rock and ice rising to impossible heights, and he would struggle to remember when and where he'd seen them.

On one occasion, just a few days after the Amethyst Mountain hike, he awoke in a sweat, heart racing, to find his mother seated beside him on the bed, silhouetted by the light in the hall.

"You okay, Sweetie?" she asked. "You were talking in your sleep—and yelling a little, too."

Andrew scooched back against his pillow and stared at the ceiling, trying to remember. "We were stuck in the snow," he whispered, still half asleep. "And there was something bad on the other side."

His mother looked at him curiously. In the darkened room, he could see the glint of her eyes but not much else. "Other side of what?" she asked.

Andrew kept his eyes fixed on the ceiling. A sliver of light from the hall formed a dagger-like pattern that he found disquieting.

"I don't know," he said. "It didn't make sense."

She stroked his forehead and touched his cheek— her hand cool and reassuring on his face. He could feel his heart rate slowing, settling down. He felt a little silly. He was eleven years old—too old for comforting, he thought. But he was glad she was there all the same.

His mother sat beside him in silence for a long time, so long that he started to drift back to sleep.

"What happened to you guys?" she asked, her soft voice summoning him back to wakefulness. "On that hike you took with your daddy?"

Andrew thought about it. "We ran into a snowstorm," he whispered. "And the roads were already bad."

She watched him. "That's what your daddy says. But he seemed rattled when he got home."

Andrew wasn't sure how to reply. He shrugged.

"It takes a lot to rattle Malcolm Liggett," his mom said.

Andrew had a fleeting memory of his father walking away from him on the summit of Amethyst Mountain. Walking from white into green. From a winter blizzard into spring. The memory made no sense.

"We got a little lost," he said, turning to her in the dark. "But I had my compass."

His mother smiled. "I'm glad about that," she said. She sat beside the boy, watching him and holding his hand until he drifted back to sleep. "I love you," she whispered, leaning close to kiss his forehead.

On another occasion, during high school while looking for things to donate to an auction in support of his track team, Andrew rediscovered the old geology book on a high shelf and the flower hidden inside. The discovery froze him in place and flooded his mind with an instantaneous and inexplicable rush of disparate emotions—sadness, longing, fear, joy. He'd stared at the desiccated flower—still a vivid red—for what seemed like hours, abandoning the day's other commitments, trying only to recall where he'd seen the thing before, knowing somehow that the full memory, the whole story, was right there, buried in his head, just out of reach. He sat, straining to remember. After a time, though, he'd given up, closed the book, and returned it to the shelf, forgetting it again almost as soon as he put it away.

A word about the author…

Kenneth G. Bennett is the author of the sci-fi thriller *Exodus 2022* and the young adult novels *The Gaia Wars* and *Battle for Cascadia*. Ken's young adult sci-fi wilderness thriller, *Lost Boy*, will be published in 2022, and his adult paranormal thriller, *The Territory*, is due in 2023. Ken lives with his wife, Susan, an artist and marine naturalist, on an island in the Pacific Northwest.